GRADUATION IN RED

OTHER BOOKS IN THE ARGOSY LIBRARY:

THE BLOOD TRAIL: THE COMPLETE CASES
OF MORTON & McGARVEY, VOLUME 2
DONALD BARR CHIDSEY

GRADUATION IN RED
B.B. FOWLER

THE YIN SHEE DRAGON: THE COMPLETE
CASES OF MIKE & TRIXIE, VOLUME 2
T.T. FLYNN

THE WILD MAN OF CAPE COD
FRED MACISAAC

THREE GUNS FOR TONTO: THE COMPLETE
TALES OF SHERIFF HENRY, VOLUME 7
W.C. TUTTLE

HELL'S BACKYARD: THE COMPLETE
CASES OF TUG NORTON, VOLUME 2
EDWARD PARRISH WARE

MURDERER'S PARADISE: THE COMPLETE
ADVENTURES OF SINGAPORE SAMMY, VOLUME 4
GEORGE F. WORTS

ALWAYS OBEY ORDERS: THE F.V.W. MASON
FOREIGN LEGION STORIES OMNIBUS, VOLUME 2
F.V.W. MASON

POISONED HARMONY: THE COMPLETE CASES
OF THE SCIENTIFIC CLUB, VOLUME 2
RAY CUMMINGS

THE STUFFED MEN: THE COMPLETE CASES
OF JIGGER MASTERS, VOLUME 3
ANTHONY M. RUD

GRADUATION IN RED

B.B. FOWLER

COVER BY
V.E. PYLES

POPULAR PUBLICATIONS · 2023

TABLE OF CONTENTS

GRADUATION IN RED

THE STRANGE YOUNG MAN 3
REVELATION OF IDENTITY 12
VOICE FROM THE PAST 21
GANGSTERS ARE RATS. 31
NO FRIENDS ALLOWED 40
THE LEGION OF PALADINS 51
THE FAT MAN 61
ROLY-POLY DYNAMITE 71
NATIONAL CRISIS. 80
FEAR RAMPANT 92
CONTACT 96
IMP OF SATAN 105
THE BIG SLOB 113
HIDE-OUT 120
TRAIL OF RED 126
MASS HYSTERIA 132
BREAKING AND ENTERING 139
WILL O'THE WISP 145
THE TRAP. 154
DISASTER 159
THE HOODED MAN 164
THE UPPER ROOM 172
GETAWAY 178

SUBSTITUTE PRESIDENT 186

BRISSON MEETS JUSTICE 195

THE WAY OUT 201

GRADUATION IN RED

*Years of Careful Coaching Had Made Barry
Chase the Most Efficient Man-Hunter in
History; Ten Minutes of Gunfire Launched
Him on His Crime-Fighting Career*

1

THE STRANGE YOUNG MAN

ALL THAT HE knew about himself was that he was twenty-four years old and was called Barry Chase. He knew, also, that Barry Chase wasn't his right name. It was, he felt, just the name the gray man had given him. But some day he would know his right name. Some day he would find out who he was and why he had been trained as he had been the last dozen years. The gray man would tell him. He had promised that, and Barry trusted the gray man implicitly.

He sat as motionless as the rock beside him. He sat so that a spruce limb shaded his face, made it indistinguishable. His khaki shirt and trousers took care of the rest of his body. He knew that he merged perfectly into the background of foliage as long as he did not move. Long years of practice had equipped him with the ability to remain absolutely motionless for hours at a time; for hours in which not a muscle stirred. But, though muscles did not quiver, he was as alert as a coiled snake. His gray eyes watched the forest that flowed down the slopes of the opposite hill. When a movement occurred he would see it and mentally note its location and manner of motion. It was part of the game that went on everlastingly through its different phases.

In a tiny patch of clearing he saw a tree that hadn't been there a few moments before. He watched it. He could see

*Barry leaped for the
machine gunner.*

no perceptible motion. But the dwarf pine had appeared on one edge of the clearing, and later, without seeming to have moved, it was at the other side. He watched a jay leap in startled alarm. Even at that distance he could hear perfectly its raucous scolding, as it flew around this strange tree that moved.

Anyone watching him would have marveled. His bronzed young face had something of Indian stoicism in its impassivity. The chin was strong, the mouth wide, firm and mobile. His eyes were grayish under a straight slash of brows. They were eyes that seemed to look through whatever they rested upon. Anyone so studying him would have guessed his age as about twenty-four. But at the same time he would have been baffled by the alert concentration, the gravity and wisdom that was almost ageless.

Barry was thinking of the past that had made him what he was, while he watched the opposite hillside. That was

The hoodlum was unaware of the silent Indian who crept toward him.

another trick he had learned in the years behind him. He could let a section of his brain go off on mental quests and excursions while he retained full possession and control of every faculty; nose trained to pick up foreign scents with the sure sensitivity of a bird dog; ears that detected sounds that were inaudible to the untrained ear; eyes that missed nothing; muscles always ready to launch him into instant and coordinated action. All this had become a part of him.

Just now he was trying to remember something that forever eluded him. There had been a woman whose face he sometimes saw in his sleep, a pale oval of loveliness with wide, dark eyes and a smile that made him tremble a little. There was a memory of arms, too; arms that enfolded a child and brought a sense of shelter and comfort he had never known.

There was a man, too. He could recall the adoring eyes of

a man when he looked at the woman. The man was tall and straight with gray eyes and chin like granite. His mouth was hard, but it could curve in a smile that Barry fought always to remember.

It was at that point that vision took on nightmare qualities. He remembered a night that always made him turn cold inside. He would have shuddered if his training had not taught him perfect control of nerves. It was the memory of that night that made his face prematurely grave and hard. He often woke up in the night perspiring, with the barking roar of guns in his ears and the screams of the woman. Then the man's voice broken with mingled rage and grief. Then more guns and silence.

HE REMEMBERED BEING carried away in a man's arms; in the arms of a man who ran through alleys and kept a hard hand over his mouth to stop him from screaming. The man was sobbing as he ran. Barry knew now that man was Bill Cleghorn. There was a vivid memory of days and nights of riding on buses and trains with him.

But the first actual memory was that of the tiny house in Kansas City. Bill looked after him. The gray man used to come often. It was there that his training had begun. It started with childish games calculated to sharpen his senses and develop his physique. The gray man used to watch him with eyes that glowed strangely in their deep sockets.

Then one day the gray man had come and taken them away. They had traveled great distances to come here to the mountains. Then the real training began. The gray man had at that time made his only reference to the past. He had told the boy that wicked men had killed his father and mother and would have killed him. He must make himself ready for the day he should strike back at them. To that end he was being trained.

That goal was always before him. But he wasn't impatient. For part of his training had been in patience. He had been drilled in the cold and unfaltering patience of the hunter, knowing that it is only by patience that the game is won.

Of the gray man he knew no more than the day he had come here with him. To the first childish questions the gray man presented an impenetrable mask. He called the gray man Uncle Dirk, believed that he was really an uncle, but always thought of him as the gray man.

A man stepped clear of the forest and waved his arms. The man was tall, naked to the waist, his skin like dark bronze. A flicker of satisfaction touched the gray eyes. The signal meant that the man on the opposite slope had not been able to spot him. In Barry's mind was the list of things he had observed, the signs and motions of the Indian's stealthy journey across the face of the hill.

As he looked, the Indian was gone. That was one trick Joe had perfected. One moment he would be beside you, the next he would be gone, melted somewhere into whatever shadow or cover existed.

Barry walked along the trail to the valley floor with long, lithe, soundless strides.

The spring of the Indian from behind a scrub pine was as swift as the pounce of a leopard at a waterhole. At the same instant Bill Cleghorn leaped from the tree over his head.

Barry was not there. With the first flicker of motion he was in action. His open palm stopped Joe in mid-spring, whirling him around and tossing him to the side of the trail. Barry whirled like a great cat from under Bill's fall, caught one of the long arms and flipped him into a helpless knot. The hold Barry had on him could have broken his arm. Bill knew it. Joe knew it as Barry faced him, holding Bill, waiting for Joe to get to his feet.

Joe's bronze impassivity did not crack. He stopped and slowly straightened. But deep in his black eyes there was a gleam of satisfaction.

"Excellent!" he said. "A most creditable performance." The accent from the bronzed, half-naked Indian was incongruous. But Joe, when he wasn't being the wood-en-faced, stolid, grunting Indian, used the accent that one of the big eastern universities had given him.

Bill got up, rubbing one long arm. Bill was wide of shoulder, long-armed. His short legs made him look squat and awkward. But Barry knew that he could move with ferocious speed and precision when he wished. His hands were big-knuckled and huge. They, too, looked awkward, but Barry had seen those hands handle a gun with the same uncanny skill that a magician handles a card.

As they walked along the trail, Barry gave his account of the movements he had observed. Indian Joe nodded. "Splendid." He turned to Bill and said, "The boy is about ready to graduate, don't you think?"

Bill grunted noncommittally. His pale eyes told nothing. "Maybe. We'll let the chief decide that."

Deep inside Barry knew that he was ready to graduate. He was ready for the job that lay before him. He had sensed it in the attitude of his teachers for some time. The fight two weeks ago had told him that.

A few days before that fight the gray man had told him that he had been matched to fight Slasher Burke, the heavyweight who had been shooting up through the ranks of contenders like a destroying gale. He had been trained for that for years. Since he was twelve he had been trained by mysterious men brought in by the gray man. Those men had taught him to fight, to box and wrestle. They had instructed him in the dirty tactics of roughhouse fighting. And always before him was the woman's face, her screams in his ears. His muscles as fluid as oil, as tough as whip cord, he had come to the point where the men who were brought in were not matches for him. Then the big fight at Iron town.

HE HAD TAKEN on the job as he had taken all others: eagerly, yet coldly sure and precise in his movements. For five rounds he only used his left. He was obeying orders. In the sixth Bill had told him to cut loose, so he had knocked the dreaded Slasher Burke cold with two devastating punches.

The gray man was waiting for them when they got to the lodge that nestled against the bluff at the edge of the wide clearing. He was gray of hair. His skin was a lifeless gray. His eyes were gray, keen, bleak and cold. He said curtly to Barry, "Go in and get ready for lunch. Carpenter is waiting for you."

Carpenter was the little man with rabbitty eyes and the mouse-colored hair. In repose he was a nonentity, mild, colorless. Barry guessed that some time Carpenter had been a great actor. He was a master at the art of make-up and characterization. Barry had seen him turn his mild countenance into a devil's mask. He had seen him register such brutality, horror, imbecility or comedy at will that in earlier days Barry had marveled. Now, after years of instruction in the art, he no longer marveled but emulated.

Today he sat down before the mirror and began his make-up. Carpenter's soft voice instructed him. "You are an escaped killer. You are trying to keep up a front but inwardly you are seething with terror, black hatred, viciousness. You naturally try to fool those you meet and give yourself away at the same time. Go ahead."

Trained muscles in Barry's face relaxed here, tightened there. His mobile mouth twisted in a snarl of vicious fury. He touched his lower lids subtly with make-up and the eyes became red-rimmed, the expression in the gray eyes changed. They became narrow, glittering, craven and threatening at the same time.

When he got up from the mirror he carefully dressed the part. He walked out to the table where the others were sitting down. He slumped in his chair, rested his tensely crooked hands on the cloth and snarled: "Come on, don't I eat in this dump? Pass the chow." His voice was hard and rasping.

The gray man said casually, "The shirt doesn't match. Either it should be cleaner or the coat dirtier. Watch things like that."

Barry turned his twisted face on him and said, "Nerts to you!"

He did not shed his character until he left the table and entered the room where he removed his make-up. This luncheon game was played every day. Sometimes he was a sailor ashore and broke. At other times he was a truck driver looking for a job, a panhandler, a happy drunk, a

hophead. Sometimes Carpenter made him stay in character day after day for months on end until he had mastered
every nuance of expression, every trick of carriage, every
gesture and accent. Barry liked it. It was a fascinating part
of the great game.

After lunch he went with Bill and Joe to the pistol range
at the other side of the clearing. For an hour he practiced
shooting. It wasn't blazing away at a target. He used different weight guns from all angles. He shot from the hip.
He fired under his arm. He closed his eyes and fired at
the sounds that Bill made as he jerked the strings of the
different targets.

Guns in his hands came alive. Bill had taught him all of
his uncanny skill. The long drills, day after day all through
the years, made him shoot as swiftly and accurately as he
thought.

Today the practice lasted less than half an hour. Bill
seemed to be nursing deep and satisfying pleasure. He
unbent so far as to lay a hand on Barry's shoulder.

"You know all that I can teach you," he said. "As far as
I'm concerned, you're ready."

2

REVELATION OF IDENTITY

THE THRILL OF secret elation followed Barry as he walked to the cave under the bluff. He dropped the curtain behind him and slid sideways along the cave wall. Somewhere in the darkness Joe was waiting for him. Joe would keep moving. That was the rule of this game. Both men must keep in action.

The test of skill lay in the sureness of motion, the sharp alertness of ears and nose, and another sense that was unexplainable. Sometimes in the inky blackness of the cave Barry felt as though he were hearing with his skin. It was as though he absorbed sound and sensation through his pores. He couldn't have explained it otherwise.

He felt a tiny stone grate under his foot and ducked low, sliding sideways as he went down. He heard the tiny plop of the pellet on the cave wall and smiled. Here in the darkness he allowed himself the luxury of a smile.

He heard the touch of Joe's shoulder against the rock wall. To the ordinary ear it would have been inaudible. But to Barry it was sharp and clear and distinct. He shot the pellet from his hand with the registery of the sound in his ear. There was no hesitation, no pause between hearing and action. He heard the pellet slap against bare flesh and smiled again.

For over an hour the game went on, weaving through the big cave, through darkness that was so thick it seemed to flow about them like dark water. There were artificial obstructions in the cave. To touch one was to lose a point. Barry had to keep in his brain at all times the clear picture of where an obstruction was in relation to the others. Each day the contestants were allowed a minute's study of the layout before the curtain dropped. After that his brain and ears and the other subtler sense became his eyes.

When the curtain lifted Barry was poised to throw his seventh pellet. He walked outside with Joe and looked at him. There were two red splashes on Joe's chest where the pellets had struck him. There was another on his right arm and one on his cheek.

"Only two misses," Joe said. "Splendid!"

Barry glanced down. There was one red splash on his shirt front and one on his trousers leg. "I threw five," Joe said ruefully.

From the caves, Barry went back to the library where the gray man waited for him. In that library he had absorbed all the knowledge that Joe had gotten in his university training. He had amplified it by reading. The gray man had added to and filled it out.

The gray man said abruptly, "I really am your uncle, Barry."

Barry nodded and the gray man went on: "Perhaps I'm superstitious, but somehow I feel that the end of my life is near. Oh, I know you are ready. You would be starting your mission soon in any case. But I have a strange sense of impending disaster. So I have decided to tell you a few things you should know."

The gray man spread a handful of yellowed newspaper clippings out on the table in front of him. He said slowly, "Gerald Sanderson, your father, was my only brother." His voice was even and steady.

He pushed a photograph toward Barry. Barry felt his pulses quicken. He recognized it as the woman whose face appeared in his dreams. But he did not let his face mirror anything of his emotion.

The gray man pushed a newspaper clipping after the photograph. Barry read the account of the marriage of Gerald Sanderson to Greta Dalbert, beautiful young debutante.

BARRY READ THE other clippings slowly. It told of the spectacular rise of Gerald Sanderson as a fighting prosecutor. He had fought the gangs that mushroomed up following the war. He had won respect and admiration by his courageous war upon the underworld.

Then Barry read the account of the murder of his father and his lovely young wife. The disappearance of Dirk Sanderson and the child was a baffling mystery.

Barry laid the clippings down with a steady hand. The gray man went on steadily: "All large scale criminal organizations are the same. They must be backed by powerful forces, who can swing influence to protect them. There must be brains to plan their campaigns and perfect their control of the underworld. Your father was after the man who stood behind the scenes. If he could reach him he could strike the world of crime a terrific blow."

The gray man's hands clenched. That was his only sign

of emotion. "He was getting very close to that man. He received threats. His own friends—and he had some loyal friends—tried to persuade him to go easy. But he drove ahead. Then it happened." The gray man's voice sunk to a whisper.

"Bill Cleghorn was your father's most trusted man. He was young then. But he always had an old head on his shoulders. He knew that the man at the top wanted to wipe us all out. Yes, you and I as well as your father. For there was a big family fortune. With us dead that fortune was to go to one of the big foundations. As long as you and I lived that fortune would be spent to bring him to justice. He knew me and knew the stuff the Sandersons were made of. So he tried to make a clean sweep.

"Sometimes you must have wondered what this train-ing was for. I have told you only the barest outlines in the past. Just enough to make you stick to your training. Now you are equipped as no other man is equipped. And you'll need all of that. For when you go to New York you will be hunted night and day by men who will kill you the moment they find you. You must beat them. You must drive through them all to find the man who heads their organization."

He fixed Barry with his bleak eyes. "Until then you must be a man without any name. You cannot claim your name and fortune until that man is found and exposed. Make no mistake. Before that time you cannot be Gerald Sand-erson."

The gray man got up and paced the room slowly. "When you leave here no man must know your secret. Trust no one. No matter how much you may be attracted to anyone, man or woman, you must not trust that person. If you do, one of two things will happen. That person will inadvertently let drop something that will be your ruin. Or your friendship with that person will become known, and they will strike at you through your friends."

He paused and fixed Barry with his icy stare. "Can you do that? Can you go through the years without friends, turning your back on love, companionship? Can you keep your counsel at all times?"

Barry said firmly, "I can!"

The gray man said: "I know you can. I am telling you this to fix the necessity for silence and aloofness on your mind."

He crossed to the safe and took from it a long black box. He opened it. "In this box," he told Barry, "is ten thousand in currency. There is a key also. That key belongs to a safety deposit box in New York. There is another ten thousand there. That isn't much for what you have to do. But by the time it's gone, you will know the crime ring in New York. When you need more take it from them. Make them pay your expenses."

Barry asked but one question. "Do I go back to New York alone?"

"I DON'T KNOW," the gray man said slowly. "I had always planned that we five should go back together and scatter through the city. Joe and Bill know some of the men left in the gangs. What they don't know they can find out. But they also might be discovered. I would be almost surely discovered. So I could not remain close to you. Carpenter, of course, could become a different man. So could Joe. He has a few tricks of disguise that are as good as Carpenter's."

He ran his thin fingers through his gray hair and his eyes were brooding. "But somehow I feel that the end is near for me. I don't know why it is, but I can't get away from it. So, if you must go alone, stay alone. Trust no one if we who have taught you are taken away from you."

Barry walked out of the library later into the dying afternoon with a cold hand on his heart. At the same time his pulses were pounding with the import of what he had heard. But outwardly he was as cold and impassive as ever.

He walked away from the house and sat down at the edge of the clearing. He went over the story the gray man had told him and felt bitter rage blow like an icy breeze through his heart. He was ready for the blood chase. He would hunt the unknown boss of crime as relentlessly as ever a panther stalked a fawn.

But even as his brain worked his faculties were as keen and alert as ever. They worked independent of his thinking. Without turning his head he said: "Come out, Joe. I heard you when you left the house. I heard you when you let a fir branch brush your shoulder a moment ago. Come on out."

Joe drifted soundlessly from the shelter of the scrub pine and squatted on his heels beside Barry. He chuckled briefly. Then he stared across the clearing with his brooding eyes. "Did Dirk tell you?" he asked.

Barry nodded. Joe went on: "I guess you leave us then. I guess you graduate now. I hope it's in the cards for me to go with you. I could help." His bronze face twitched. "I guess I'm a hell of an Indian," he said dryly. "When I think of us busting up I get all mushy inside."

Gazing over the hills Barry was thinking of the glorious days he had spent with Joe. He thought of days in the woods when the two had stalked their game in the primitive fashion. He had seen Joe stalk a deer to kill it with a knife. And then Barry had duplicated the feat. Those days were poignant in his memory. He put a hand on Joe's shoulder and let it rest there. That was the only sign he allowed himself to make.

Bill came out on the porch and yelled, "Dinner's most ready." So the two of them got up and walked silently to the lodge.

In the house Barry dressed carefully. He put on his evening dress and donned his character at the same time. He was an affected young bounder. His mouth and eyes were vacuous. He talked with an affected drawl. His shoulders drooped and he walked with awkward laziness. He made a picture of an over-pampered, over-indulged son of wealth.

When Joe waited on him he complained pettishly over the service. He ate and complained over the food in fatuous ill-humor.

Bill, who had cooked the food, stood in the kitchen door and beamed. Joe, waiting in soft-footed servility on the table, bowed and whined his regrets with a pleased light in his eyes. Carpenter watched the performance with no expression on his face. The gray man studied him narrowly. When the meal was finished he said, tersely, "You'll do."

Carpenter said in his mild voice: "A perfect performance."

IT WAS DARK when Barry—out of his evening dress and back in his khaki shirt and trousers with rubber-soled tennis shoes on his feet—said to Joe, "I'd like to hike over the cone tonight."

Joe said, "You're on. Let's go."

On the peak of the cone-shaped hill they squatted

on their heels and stared out over the slopes and valleys beneath them. Neither of them spoke. Both were intent on what they could hear and sense below them.

The squeal of a rabbit, as a weasel pounced upon it a mile away, came to Barry clearly and distinctly. He could hear the beat of a bird's wings as an owl swooped down and picked it from its poorly chosen roost. The woods were alive with small rustlings of wild life, the woods dwellers scurrying for food, fighting for survival, weaving the interminable tale of existence.

An hour later they both stood up and headed for the lodge without a word. They had walked a few hundred yards when Joe said softly: "I'm an Indian, Barry, and Indians get strange hunches. I feel as if I could hear the sky getting ready to fall. There's something in the wind. I can smell it as I can smell a storm two days before it appears."

Barry said nothing. But he was thinking of the presentiment that had driven the gray man to talk to him today.

They were almost to the clearing when they heard the machine gun. It pounded with hammers of brass on the black iron doors of night. It woke thunderous echoes that rolled tremendously toward the silent stars. Both men stopped, frozen.

Joe was the first to speak. His voice was thin and bleak. "They've caught up with us at last. I guess that's what I felt."

Barry said: "We have no guns with us. We're better off without them tonight. You circle the lodge and come up on them on the other side. I'll take this side."

Then he was standing alone. Joe had vanished as silently as if the night had swallowed him. Barry went on as silently as a shadow.

He stood briefly at the edge of the clearing. He could see the man with the machine gun spitting orange jets into the darkness. At the corner of the house a gun barked twice and the machine gunner folded up across his gun. Then Barry saw another man crawl out and pull the gun from beneath the dead man.

A man farther over flung something and yelled hoarsely, "I guess that will fix him." Searing flame spouted like a fountain at the base of the big pine beyond the house. In the core of it Barry saw a man dissolving. Then silence pressed down like a hand upon the explosion.

Barry felt cold at his heart. That was Bill.

There were no other shots. The man with the machine gun said hoarsely, "We got three of them! There are two more. One of them is the young guy. We've got to get him!"

As he spoke Barry was upon him. He caught the man's chin in one hand, cupped the back of the bullet head in the steel fingers of the other. He put a knee in the middle of the man's back as he twisted his head.

The man uttered one strangled yelp and collapsed, his head at a horrible angle on his broken neck. At the other side of the clearing a man screamed once, high-pitched and terrible. Then the scream broke and died in a gurgling moan.

A man came running forward. He had a gun in one hand, a gleaming cylinder in the other. He almost fell over the dead machine gunner, bent down and threw the beam of his flashlight in the dead man's face.

Another voice across the clearing said: "Put that damned light out! What the hell are you askin' for?"

3

VOICE FROM THE PAST

AS THE LIGHT snapped off, Barry went forward in the darkness. His right hand came around and down as the man started to straighten up. The man dropped without a sound. Barry knew that the man was dead. The impact of the edge of his hand on the man's neck had snapped the vertebrae.

He squatted on his heels and chirped. From the darkness came an answering chirp. Joe put his head down and Barry whispered: "Bring the man you got over to the car." He pointed to the blotch of blackness against the woods.

He picked a man up in each hand and carried them over. He dropped them in front of the car and stepped back as someone came running across the clearing. The man was panting heavily as he ran. Barry moved to the car, put one hand in the window and took out the ignition key as Joe dumped the man he carried with the other two.

The man who was running was joined by another. The voice of the second man was thick with fear. "This damn place is spooky," he blurted. "I don't like it!"

The second man spoke harshly: "Shut up, you fool! Where's Baldy and Prince?"

The man sobbed: "I don't know! Baldy was in the clearing when I chucked the pineapple at the guy behind the tree. Then he disappeared like the ground had swallowed him."

Barry saw the flash of the knife as it left Joe's hand. It caught the self-confessed killer of Bill in the throat.

The other man inched toward the car door. He eased it open and slid in behind the wheel, reaching for the ignition key. Barry's voice jolted him erect.

"I have the key," he said. "Get out of the car."

The man dived out of the car, the gun in his hand blasting in the direction of the voice. Barry and Joe were not there then. They ran lightly around the car.

When he spoke again Barry was less than a dozen yards from the man. His voice was as cold as the flow of water over ice. "You damned fool," he said thinly. "If I had wanted to kill you I could have done so a dozen times. I have a gun in my hand, see?" He blasted two slugs past the man's ear into the body of the car.

"I could have put those in your heart just as easily as in the car," he said thinly on the echoes. "Drop that gun!"

He heard the thump of the gun on the ground and said, "Now snap on the headlights."

The beams of the headlights made a wide swath of white brilliance across the clearing. In the light Barry could see someone lying on the porch steps, and he guessed that would be the gray man.

At the same instant the man in the car saw the three dead men piled up in front of the car. Barry's voice said relentlessly, "Pick up the three of them and throw them in the back. Chuck that man beside you in also." Without turning his head he said, "Joe, get the man that Bill shot and drag him over here."

When the five men were in the car Barry asked, "Is that all of them?"

The man at the car said in husky whisper, "Yes."

"Go and stand in front of the headlights!" His voice cracked like a whip as the man hesitated. "Go on if you don't want to die now."

The man stood in the blazing light. He was tall and gaunt. His face was long and narrow. At Barry's elbow Joe whispered softly: "Trigger Gorman. Ex-con. Killer."

BARRY WENT ON, "Now, Gorman, when you get in the car, drive back to whoever sent you and tell him what happened. You killed my friends. For that I'm going to kill with as little compunction as he uses. Tell him there's no hole deep enough to hide him; no darkness black enough to shelter him from me."

He could see Gorman shiver with the impact of his words. "That goes for you, too, Gorman. You'll die for your work tonight. I promise you that. I'm letting you go now only because I want you to carry word to the man who hired you. Here's your ignition key. Go!"

The key made a glittering arc through the headlight beam to fall af Gorman's feet. Gorman picked it up and backed toward the car. He got in, whirled the starter, wheeled the car around and headed for the road that led out from the clearing. Barry stood watching until the red tail-light was swallowed by the woods.

The gray man was lying on the steps. He must have run out when he heard the car. Carpenter was on the porch. He had probably come out with the gray man and caught part of the same burst of fire. Bill, Barry reasoned, had been away from the house. He had taken cover behind a tree and had been blasted out by the grenade. Neither Barry nor Joe spoke while then gathered up what they could find of Bill in a blanket.

Barry's hand was steady as he lifted the receiver. His voice was also steady as he called the state police and reported what had happened. All through the days that followed he was calm and cool. The police came, their men guarding the clearing while they investigated. Barry gave them the license number of the car. It had been discovered, the back seat bathed in blood, discarded on a side road. Of the men who had been in the back they found nothing. The car had been stolen in New York.

ONE AFTERNOON BARRY squatted on the porch beside Joe. They were protected by an angle of the house from two men at the edge of the woods. The men made Barry feel faintly contemptuous. They thought they were hidden and had given themselves away a dozen times.

Joe spoke first. "I guess it's time for us to blow."

Barry nodded his head toward the woods. "We'll talk to those fellows first. Probably they know where their boss hangs out."

Joe said, "Hired killers brought in to finish the job. I imagine even their boss is an underling."

Barry said, "Perhaps. But he was responsible for the killing of the others."

Barry stood up. "I'll go in and start to pack a few things. You watch."

He was packing a trunk with clothes when Joe said softly, "A car just turned in off the main road."

Barry came back to the porch to stand in the protected angle of the house. He closed his eyes to concentrate more effectively. "It's a high-powered car." He listened again. "It's not the one that was here before."

He was silent a moment and then said, "It's an open car. I can hear two people talking as they drive, a man and a woman."

Joe nodded. "Fine," he said. "You've been trained well." Then he amplified what Barry had told him. "The woman is young. The man is much older, judging from his voice." He shifted the gun under his armpit, hidden by the loose jacket he wore, and said to Barry, "Better go inside in case it's just a trick to get close. Stay inside. I'll take care of this end."

Barry saw the wisdom of Joe's advice. He went back into the living room and waited. He heard the girl's clear, bright voice. He heard the car purr across the clearing and come to a stop before the porch. He could hear the creak of the leather upholstery as someone got out of the seat. Then he heard the man's voice, mellow, deep and vibrant:

"Is Gerald Sanderson here?"

JOE SAID STOLIDLY, "Nobody by that name lives here, mister. Better go where you come from."

The man's voice said: "I mean the young man who lives here. Perhaps you don't know him by that name."

Joe's voice was guttural, wooden. "You mean Mr. Barry Chase. He inside. You go in."

Feet climbed the porch steps. One pair light and springy, the other heavy and firm. Barry stood inside the door. His voice was mildly pleasant.

"Anything I can do for you?"

The man was tall and straight. His eyes were clear and

fine. His iron-gray hair was brushed back from a magnificent forehead. His mouth was neither too hard nor too lax. But it was the girl who gripped Barry's eyes. He had never seen anything like her. She was without a hat. The sunlight behind her made her hair a glory of burnished bronze. Her eyes were deep, deep blue and looked at Barry frankly and levelly. Her mouth was adorable.

The gray man's warning beat through his mind. No matter how you may be attracted to anyone, man or woman, you must not trust that person. Barry's face was the habitual impassive mask. His courtesy was only surface as he said, "Won't you come in?"

When they were inside the man said, "Don't you know that you are Gerald Sanderson?" He went on: "I know. I've had detectives looking for you down through all these years since you were taken away. They connected the recent murders here with you."

Barry said evenly, "I've lived here for several years. My name is Barry Chase."

"You are Gerald Sanderson," the man continued. "Don't be afraid of me. I'm Frederick Moreland. I was your father's best friend. I'd know you anywhere. You are the image of your father."

Barry's face gave no hint of emotion that touched him. "There must be some mistake," he said politely. "I am Barry Chase."

The girl stepped forward, hand thrust out and said, impulsively, warmly, "You must trust Uncle Fred. I know how he has searched for you. He promised your father long ago that if anything happened he would look out for you."

Her voice was like her eyes, clear and true. "Uncle Fred is your friend. Won't you trust us?"

Barry smiled, a smile that curved his lips, touched his eyes but told nothing. His voice was more polite than ever as he took her hand and bowed over it. "I am really sorry. If you offer Barry Chase your friendship I can accept it. But I could not accept it as one I am not."

The girl's face was like a playground for her feelings. Her lips pouted. Shadows crossed the shining clarity of her eyes. Then the eyes went cold as if under a deep cloud. She withdrew her hand and said, "I'm sorry."

Moreland broke in: "This is Elsa Darrow, my niece. I know you are Gerald Sanderson. Why won't you admit it and come back to New York with us?"

"I am really sorry," Barry went on in the same well-modulated voice, "but I must disappoint you. I am Barry Chase. Sometime I would be delighted to call upon you in New York if you will allow me to call as Barry Chase."

MORELAND SHOOK HIS head slowly. "You grieve me, my boy." Then he brightened. "Stick to your name for the present, if you wish. If you do come to New York look me up, whatever your name."

Barry stood inside the door as they went out. "I shall be delighted."

He stood on the porch, still sheltered by the angle of the house. The girl smiled as she reached the bottom step. "Aren't you going to come down and see me into the car?"

Barry's eyes were very bleak then. He couldn't but believe that this girl was to be trusted. But he knew of the men who waited. Beside him Joe stirred slightly.

"Under other circumstances," Barry said smoothly, "I

should be delighted to carry out my duties as host. But if I were to step down there now I should never return to this porch alive."

Moreland froze into shocked unbelief. The girl gasped. "What do you mean?" she asked indignantly.

Barry smiled. "Turn and look at the woods and tell me if you see anything."

The girl stared, shaking her head. Then she asked, "Do you see anything?"

"From where I stand," Barry said calmly, "I can see two men. They think they are hidden but a dozen signs give them away. I can see the face of one as he peers between two fir branches. I see the glint of the sun on the rifle of the other. I can hear them talking."

Incredulity touched the girl's eyes. "I suppose," she said sarcastically, "you can hear what they are saying?"

Barry smiled. "Joe, tell them what you hear."

Joe said woodenly: "Big man looking through trees says you are not coming out. Little man says if you do he will plug you what he calls 'dead center.' Big man now chuckling."

Moreland frowned in blank incredulity. "Do you expect us to believe that you can hear two men talking over that distance?"

Barry's polite smile touched his lips again. "As you came out into the clearing in your car," he told them, "the young lady said quite distinctly. 'Are you sure that this is the man you are looking for?' You answered that you were positive."

Moreland gasped. The girl's eyes were wider and darker as she asked, "How are you able to hear so clearly?"

Barry said lightly, "Matter of training. I have been very well trained."

Moreland stared at him long and steady before he climbed into the car. "You are a most remarkable young man, Gerald Sanderson."

Barry said, "Pardon me. Barry Chase. Good afternoon." He stood and watched the car cross the clearing.

Joe said, "It's strange no one made any attempt to stop them."

"Probably hoped I'd go back with them and give them their chance," Barry answered. He went slowly to his packing.

A few minutes later Joe called, "Barry!" To Barry's trained ears the note of interest and mingled excitement was noticeable under the calm surface.

At the door Barry asked, "Yes?"

"The car stopped at the main road," Joe said. "I heard men's voices. The girl screamed once, then stopped abruptly. I think she got into the other car. Anyway it started down the road. Moreland's car is coming back."

Moreland leaped out of the car as he yanked on the parking brake and raced up the stairs. His eyes were scared. His face was strained. "Sanderson!" he said sharply.

"Chase, if you please."

Moreland's voice was sharp. "All right, Chase, if you insist. But this is no time for argument. Three men stopped me at the road. They were armed with a machine gun and revolvers. They forced Elsa into a car and sent me back to tell you that if you do not give yourself up to them they will kill the girl."

Barry put a smile on his lips that he did not feel. "Melodramatic in the extreme," he said smoothly. "It has all the elements of the standard plot. I had given these men credit for more imagination. Why do they think I will allow myself to be butchered to save a girl I never saw before in my life?"

"But what will we do?" Moreland blurted. "I believe them. They will kill Elsa."

"Go back," Barry said thinly, "and tell them that I refuse to give myself up now. Tell them I said that I would come to you in Grandville tonight. Tell them that you will help to trap me."

Moreland said, "You will come to Grandville? Don't you know that they will kill you?"

"They will try," Barry said calmly. "Now tell me, Mr. Moreland, where are you staying?"

Moreland said in a choked voice, "At the Garden Hotel."

"You will hear from me this evening," Barry said. "You may take my word for that."

Moreland stared at him closely. "I believe you mean it!"

"I rarely say things that I do not mean," Barry said evenly. "Until this evening, sir." He bowed. "Tell the gentlemen below that."

4

GANGSTERS ARE RATS

AFTER MORELAND HAD gone, Joe asked, "Do you think the two of them are a part of the plot to get you?"

Barry shook his head. "I don't think so." He was thinking of the girl. He couldn't believe that she was part of the gang. Her eyes would not be so fine and clear if she were. And there was something about Moreland that put him apart from these men.

Joe said as if he were thinking aloud: "Her scream down by the road was real enough. She was really frightened. It looks bad, Barry."

Barry said evenly, "We'll fix it so it looks right, this evening. When it gets dark we'll start for town."

Just before dark Joe came in to cook the evening meal. Barry squatted on his heels on the porch and watched the woods. When Joe came out to tell him that supper was ready he said pleasantly, "Our two friends have gone."

Joe lifted his eyebrows questioningly and Barry went on: "A third man joined them a moment ago. He told them that the boss had called them in; that he had a better plan for catching us. The big man was positively overcome with relief. He said that we gave him the jitters."

Joe's eyes were narrow slits as he said, "They just got out in time. I was going down to visit them before we left."

As they ate Barry added, "The car that was parked by the main road left also."

Joe said, "I'll take a look before we drive out. There may be a man posted there to take a pop shot at us."

A half hour later Joe came back. "Clean," he said tersely. "They've pulled them all in. I imagine they figure they'll need them all this evening."

As they drove through the velvety darkness an hour later Barry felt that his heart was a lump of lead in his chest. The old life was over. Three of the only four friends he had had in the world were dead. They had been a part of a fine, clean life in his beloved hills. Now he knew that the time had come when he must leave the hills and live in the cities he hated. He had to exchange the clarity and purity of the mountains for the filth and grime and smoke of towns. And he couldn't come back till his mission was accomplished. The hills would never know him again until he walked under his own name a free man upon the earth.

He threaded his way through the streets, avoiding the main thoroughfares where he might attract the attention of any of the gang who might be posted as lookouts. A few blocks from the hotel he stopped the car and said to Joe, "I'll go along to the hotel. You bring the car closer and spot them when they take me away. You can drive without lights. Trail me and do your stuff."

Joe's voice was sharp: "You can bank on that. I'll work the way we've always planned we'd work."

He was turning away when Joe put a hand on his arm. "Good hunting, *amigo*."

Barry said, "Good hunting, Joe. I'll see you at the blow-off."

Joe went on, "Be a credit to your teachers. Remember the advice all of us gave you. Never be in a hurry to strike. Strike swiftly, but never in a hurry. You've graduated."

A chill trickle ran along Barry's spine. He remembered the stains that he and Joe had tried to scrub out of the porch floor. His voice was as thin as sleet: "Graduated. Graduated in red." His face was still the impassive mask. But something in his eyes made Joe draw in his breath with a hiss.

WALKING THROUGH THE streets Barry remembered what Bill Cleghorn had always drilled into him. "Gangsters are rats. When they've got the advantage they can be vicious and merciless. Take that advantage away from them and the yellow shows. With the upper hand they're hell on wheels. On the short end they're rabbits. Always remember and manage to inject the element that gives you advantage. Fight your own way. Don't try theirs."

The thought made Barry's eyes gleam. He knew one element that he could inject tonight into the game. He had been trained in that element. He knew that Joe would do his part when the time came.

In the drug store a block from the hotel Barry called Moreland. His voice came crackling hysterically over the wire. "Chase? Where are you? Are you coming into town?"

Barry said calmly: "I am in town. I'll be at the hotel in a few minutes. That was what I promised, wasn't it? If you are in touch with the gangsters tell them I'm on my way."

Moreland's voice was thick. "One of Skelton's men in here with me now. Skelton is in hiding somewhere with the girl. His men are to take you to him." His voice faltered. "I'm hideously sorry, Chase."

"Think nothing of it," Barry's voice was light. "It's a pleasure, I assure you. I should tender you a vote of thanks for being of assistance in getting me this appointment."

"But how do we know he will keep his promise?" Moreland asked brokenly. "How do we know that Skelton will release the girl?"

"I know that is farthest from Skelton's mind," Barry said. "He wouldn't dare let either the girl or yourself live with what you know."

Moreland's gasp came to his ears and he hurried on: "But I know also that the girl will be released. I intend to bring her back to you. Tell the thug who is in your room that I am coming because I wish. Tell him that I will kill Skelton and leave the hide-out when I wish. Tell him that."

He hung up on Moreland and walked out of the drug store. At least he knew none of the men in charge here. He circled the block and entered the hotel by a side entrance. He crossed the lobby and stood for a moment staring out the front entrance, his eyes sharp and icely amused.

A sedan was at the curb, rear door open, motor running. Two men were in the hotel entrance staring up and down the street. He brought them whirling around like startled cats when he said softly, "Were you waiting for me?"

They closed in on him swiftly. Barry felt the jab of gun muzzles and smiled bleakly. "Why the melodrama?" he asked mildly. "I came here to go with you. You act as though you just made a great capture."

One of the men was slight and wiry. His eyes glittered

under the rim of a derby hat. His mouth thinned out. "You're a very wise monkey, ain't you?"

The other man was older, bigger and harder. His voice was low. "Easy, Snapper. This guy is dynamite. You heard what Gorman told the boss. We want to get him out there all in one piece."

Snapper shrugged his thin shoulders nervously. "All right. What are we waiting for? Let's get going. But if I had my way I'd pump him full of lead and leave him in a ditch outside of town."

"If you had your way," the older man drawled, "we'd all be dead and buried by now. Use your head."

SNAPPER GOT ONTO the car first. The older man prodded Barry with his gun in his pocket and followed him in. As Barry sat down Snapper smashed him across the mouth with the back of his hand. His voice was jittery with nervousness. "Hell, I think this guy is overrated."

The older man looked at Barry with his pale eyes. He shook his bony head and said, "I know he isn't. I don't like any part of this business."

Barry said nothing. He sat back in the seat, staring straight ahead at the road with eyes out of which all expression had been washed. The older man looked at his eyes again and shivered a little. Snapper laughed, but the laugh had a false ring to it.

The car ran under a canopy at the end of an old stone mansion a few miles outside of town. A man stepped out from the shadows of the doorway. He had a machine gun in his hands, held at the ready while Barry got out of the car.

He followed wordlessly on Snapper's heels through the door, across a wide entry hall and up a wide flight of stairs.

The other man walked far enough behind so Barry could not kick back and get him.

In the upper hall a door opened and someone said, "So the knight errant did turn up. How very interesting!"

Barry knew at a glance that here was a man who was made of different stuff than the other thugs he had met. He was slight and dapper. His mouth was thinly humorous. His eyes were soft and dark. But as they rested on Barry something writhed far back in their depths. His voice went on softly: "My, what a handsome brute! But hardly, I think, the mental marvel that I have been led to believe."

There were two other men in the room beside this man. One was Trigger Gorman. He came forward now, his bony shoulders stooped a little. His cheeks were hollow, his eyes burning feverishly.

"Believe me, Boss," he said earnestly, "this guy is dynamite."

Skelton stared closer. He looked long into Barry's eyes and shrugged. "I rather believe you are right, Gorman. We shall take every precaution handling this fellow whom you have billed as a human wildcat. Tie him into the chair, boys. Perhaps we can hold him then till we are ready to get rid of him."

Barry heard the girl's gasp before he saw her. Skelton had been standing between him and a glimpse of her. Now he saw that she was roped in a high-backed chair. Her bronze hair glistened in the light from the chandelier. Her eyes were wider and darker than they had been at the lodge.

Her voice was throaty. "I'm truly sorry, Mr. Chase. I am sorry that I have been used to bring you here and I'm sorry that you listened to them and came."

Barry said easily, "Not at all, Miss Darrow. It's really a pleasure. I should have come in any event."

Skelton laughed softly. "A combination Galahad and Robin Hood. A very pretty speech, Mr. Sanderson, but a trifle quixotic. You manage to put up a very brave front. But, believe me, it won't help you. The orders for your execution have been given. We have been a long time finding you. We shall make sure that we shall not have to hunt for you again."

Barry did not glance at Skelton. He knew that the dapper killer would wipe him out without compunction. But the killer did not know that Joe would be on the job. There were a lot of things that Skelton did not know. Barry remembered Bill Cleghorn's drilling.

"Remember always," Bill had told him, "that your gang-ster, however smart, lacks imagination. He credits you with the same limitations which cramp him. When they are most sure of themselves they are the easiest to beat."

WITHOUT MOVING A muscle of his face, Barry slipped the sliver of razor steel from the back of his belt. His hands were tied behind him, but trained, supple fingers, were ready to cut the cords that tied him, at a second's notice.

While he worked he listened. Skelton was watching him narrowly, speculatively. At the same time Barry knew that he was waiting for something. His ears alert to all outside sounds, Barry wondered what it was for which the man waited.

He could hear cars passing along the road. He picked each one up far down the road and followed it till it passed the house. Suddenly he stiffened. He heard the sound of a motor he recognized. He became coldly alert and tense as the car turned in the drive and stopped before the entrance downstairs. He heard the murmur of voices, knew them for sounds of three men getting out of the car. The car and the men added a new complication to the mystery. Another thing, the men below had left the motor of the car running.

Feet clumped up the stairs. Two men Barry had not seen before came into the room. Between them was Moreland. The man looked positively ill with fear. Skelton smiled at him and said, "You must have known, Moreland, that we could not release you and your niece. It was really too bad. But it's something that could not be helped."

Moreland said in a hoarse voice: "I don't care about myself. But please, if you are human, let Elsa go. I'll give you any amount of money you want. I'll do anything. Only let her go."

Skelton said, almost as if he regretted it deeply: "I'm really sorry, Mr. Moreland, but under the circumstances we have no choice in the matter."

The girl straightened in her bonds. "Don't, Uncle Fred! Don't plead for me. After all, Gerald Sanderson is the one who deserves sympathy most. He came here of his own accord to free me."

Barry said, "Pardon the correction, but the name is Chase. But I wouldn't be too tragic about it all, Miss Darrow. We're not dead yet. I, for one, do not intend to die. It is Mr. Skelton who should be most concerned at this moment."

Skelton laughed again. "I have never," he said humorously, "met a more engaging fellow." Biting mirth edged his voice. "A truly stout fellow. You know, the hero who hurls defiance into the face of the villian. 'Curse you, I fear you not, you dastard!' But it won't do, my boy. Your dramatics leave me cold." But there was in his eyes as he spoke, a shadow of something like wonder.

Skelton turned and said to the two men: "Take Moreland into the next room and stay with him. I'll tell you what to do later."

As the two men took Moreland through the door into a room beyond, Barry saw that Moreland's wrists were snapped together by handcuffs. His own hands were now free. While Skelton's back was turned Barry had cut the ropes behind him and now held the loose ends in his hands. There was only the cord around his ankles. It would be only a split second to sever that.

He had heard something else while Skelton was watching Moreland walk into the next room. At the front entrance there was a brief scurry of swift movement. He could hear a strangled gasp, the fall of a body. Two men had been at the door. They hadn't a chance with the bronzed shadow who crept up on them noiselessly and struck with the swift silence of doom.

He knew that Joe would be inside now. In a few minutes the time for action would come. Skelton turned slowly. He gazed at Barry speculatively. "I have to give you credit," he said slowly. "You have nerve. You know, of course, that you are never to leave that chair alive? We have enough respect for you not to take a single chance. You know that, don't you?"

5

NO FRIENDS ALLOWED

BARRY SAW THE cold death in Skelton's eyes. He had one hand in his pocket. Barry could see the outline of a gun there. He had to stall him for the few moments necessary to give Joe a chance. Joe was inside now. It wouldn't take him long to move.

Gorman came across the room to stand behind Skelton. The other men had guns in their hands. Their eyes were fixed on Barry. The girl's face was as pale as death, her eyes wide and dark, but she held her head proudly.

Barry lifted his head and fixed Skelton with a hard impassive stare. "I'm afraid, Mr. Skelton," he said slowly, "that you take too much for granted. It is not I who has to fear death now. It is yourself. If you but knew it you are standing in its shadow now. You will never leave this room alive. I promise you that, Skelton."

Skelton's dark eyes narrowed, his lips tightened. Barry saw the shadow of something akin to fear cross his face. He had Skelton worrying.

Skelton's lips opened to speak. He leaned forward, tense, with lust to kill in his eyes—when the overhead lights went out and darkness dropped about them like an enfolding shroud.

With the snap of the lights Barry moved. He threw himself sideways, his body twisting as the steel in his hand cut the cord at his ankles. The gun in Skelton's hand barked and a bullet sung past Barry's ear. Skelton was cool enough to have kept his nerve and fired with the drop of darkness at the place in front of him where he had seen Barry a split second before.

And now, Skelton with the gun in his hand was blasting shots into the darkness. Barry rolled soundlessly, came to his feet with the sliver of steel in his hand. He took three swift, noiseless steps and drove the slender blade through Skelton's hand. Skelton yelped as the gun thumped to the floor.

A gun across the room blasted twice and Skelton snapped, "Careful, you fool—you nearly got me that time. Take it easy. Watch that door. If anyone tries to go out, plug him."

Barry found Skelton's gun, scooped it up and dropped it into his hip pocket. He wouldn't use that now. He wanted silence. He had all the advantage now. The men in the room were afraid to fire. There was only the girl to protect. A stray bullet might hit her if one of the jittery gunmen cut loose.

Barry padded across the floor and found her chair. He slit the ropes that bound her, then touched her lips warningly with a finger. He could feel them quiver beneath his touch. He picked her up as if she were a child and carried her across the room. He had noticed a little alcove on the far side of the big fireplace. He stood her on her feet and pushed her gently back out of danger of stray bullets.

He stood for a second, as alert and poised as a stalking

panther. The shades were down so that no ray of light came into the room from outside. He listened. He could hear Skelton's hissing breath. He could picture him, standing across the room clutching his wounded hand. He could hear the breathing of the other men. It told the same story of all of them. They were ridden by terror—terror that made their breaths come in short gasps.

A few yards away a man moved. He was trying to move silently, but the scrape of his feet on the floor, the rasp of his clothes, gave him away. Barry inched nearer till the man's breath was roaring not a foot from him. Then he struck. One hand caught the man's hair and jerked his head back, the other struck him across the windpipe.

The fellow staggered back fighting for his breath. On the other side of the room a gun blasted three times. Barry heard the impact of the slugs in the man's body. Then he fell forward, his gun banging to the floor. His feet thumped twice and then he was still.

A hoarse voice said exultantly, "I got him."

Barry's voice was a thin whisper, impossible to locate in the dark. "That was one of your own men you got, my friend. I think you are next."

GORMAN'S NERVE BROKE first. "To hell with this," he bleated. "I'm pulling out." He jumped for the door. A gun across the room blasted as the door swung. For a second Barry saw Gorman outlined against the faint light that came through the door, then the gunman pitched forward.

Skelton said harshly, "That was Gorman you got, you damned fool!" He raised his voice and said, "All right, Sanderson, you've got the winning cards. How about talking business?"

He jerked convulsively as Barry whispered: "We have no business to talk, Skelton. Later, I have a few questions to ask you. I will ask those when I am ready. Just now I have to finish cleaning up."

His keen eyes detected the blur of motion that Joe made as he slipped through the open door. There was only one more gunman in the room with Skelton.

Barry stepped away from Skelton and said softly: "Here I am, you with the gun! Why not try a shot at me?"

He slid sideways as he spoke. The man in the darkness snarled as he pulled the trigger of his gun. It blasted once, as Joe's thrown knife glinted dully, then the gun banged to the floor. The man sighed deeply, sobbingly and dropped.

Joe came to stand beside Barry. "Got him," he whispered. "That leaves only Skelton and the fellows in the next room with Moreland. I took care of the two by the door before I pulled the main switch."

"Go down and throw the switch again," Barry said. "Then come back. Everything is under control now."

As Joe slid out of the room Barry said softly: "There's just the two of us now, Skelton. All of your helpers are out of the game. Remember what I told you. You were marked for death even while you gloated over me. You are like all the rest of your kind, a rat, Skelton. You have no imagination, no real intelligence. So you're going to die."

Skelton's voice was shaky. "Well," he said with the last show of bravado, "why don't you kill me and get it over with? What are you waiting for?"

Barry said softly: "Because you know things that I wish to know, Skelton. You're going to tell me about your boss, Skelton."

Skelton said, "Go to hell! I'll tell you nothing."

Barry laughed shortly. "You'll talk all right, Skelton. I know you'll talk. I know how to persuade you." Even as he spoke he could hear the throb of the motor in front. Something about it bothered him.

He was waiting for the lights when they came on in sudden brilliance. Skelton was not. He stood in the sudden glare and blinked. He was grasping his right hand, with the blood oozing between the clenched fingers. He stared at the man almost at his feet. He turned his head and saw Gorman lying across the door sill, the third man across the room. He lifted his head and stared at Barry, standing beside the fireplace, his back to the alcove where he had hidden the girl.

Barry said, "You'll talk, Skelton. You'll tell me who your boss is. You'll tell me because it is the price of your life. For I give you my word that I'll turn you loose when you tell me that one thing."

He could see in Skelton's eyes that the man was breaking.

Then Barry's nerves tautened again. He could hear the sound of swift action in the next room. A gun roared twice, a window was flung up. Then the door between the two rooms was thrown wide.

Skelton stared at the door with stark terror wiping his face of all expression. "Don't!" he screamed. "Don't!"

The blast of gunfire from the next room cut him short. Skelton flung both arms around his face as though to ward off a blow and fell forward with the arms doubled under him.

THE DOOR SLAMMED and a key clicked as Barry leaped

toward it. He put the gun in his hand against the lock and pressed the trigger. He sent slug after slug into the lock until the gun clicked. Then he threw his weight against the door. But the door was of solid material. It gave a little but did not open.

He was flinging himself against the door again when Joe came into the room and added the surge of his weight. When they burst in, Moreland was on the floor, his hands fastened behind him, blood running down his face from a gash in his forehead. Outside the motor roared and tires spun on the gravel.

Barry eased to the window and leaned out. Moreland's big open touring car hit the road at racing speed, skidded sickeningly as it hit the concrete, then roared away into the darkness. Barry could see a slender man crouched over the steering wheel, but could not get a single glimpse of his face.

He turned back into the room. Joe shook his head. "Tough luck. I passed that fellow up entirely. The boss of this outfit is very smart. He fooled us completely."

"Yes," Barry said, as he turned to Moreland to lift him to his feet. "He is smart. He was smart enough to be hidden in the case of emergency. He was smart enough to not be too sure even when he was certain he held all the cards. He was ruthless enough to kill Skelton and two gangsters in this room to keep them from talking. Anyone else alive?"

Joe said: "One of the thugs at the door. I knocked him out. I had to knife the other fellow."

"Go down and get him," Barry said tersely. "We'll see what he knows."

He turned to help Moreland, who said, brokenly, "That

one there," pointing to one of the dead men. "He put the handcuffs on me. Perhaps he has the key."

Barry found the key in the dead man's pocket, and released Moreland. Elsa had come out of the alcove and was trying to stop the flow of blood from Moreland's forehead with a handkerchief.

"Did you get a good look at the fellow?" Barry asked Moreland.

Moreland shook his head. "No," he said weakly. "He was in the room when the two men took me in there. But he was masked. He was quite slight. His hands were gloved. There was no chance to see what he looked like. When he heard you question Skelton he shot the two men who were guarding me. He struck me over the head, and threw the window open. Then he jerked the door open and fired. As soon as he had done that he locked the door and leaped through the window."

Barry said, "If I hadn't been stupid I would have gotten him. I knew they left the motor running for a reason. I should have guessed that reason."

He helped the girl make an improvised dressing for Moreland's gashed forehead. Then Joe came back with the thug who had guarded the front door. The man was shaking with abject terror as he faced Barry. In answer to the question, he said, "You can slice me to ribbons but you won't get anything from me. None of us knew who the big boss was except Skelton. We never saw him. No one but Skelton ever saw him."

Barry knew that he was telling the truth. He said tersely to Joe: "Put him in the car. You'll drive Miss Darrow and her uncle to the police station where they can tell their story. You can tell of our part in it. You, Mr. Moreland," he added, "know as much as I do about all this."

Moreland asked hoarsely, "Aren't you coming with us, Gerald?"

Barry said, "Please, the name is Barry Chase. Never forget that. No, I am not going with you. The big boss is still at large. A clever man such as he, is dangerous. I do not intend to give him another chance at me this evening. If I knew who he was I would go after him. Since I do not know, all the advantage is in his hands."

ELSA DARROW CAME to him and stretched out both her hands. "I can never thank you for what you have done," she said. "You put yourself in the hands of those horrible creatures to save my life."

Barry said evenly, "I don't like to disillusion you, Miss Darrow. But it wasn't altogether on your account that I came. By agreeing to their demand that I give myself up I was only getting in touch with the man I wanted. You thought I was taking a horrible chance. I was not. I knew what I was doing. None of these men"—he swept the figures on the floor with his bleak glance—"had a single chance."

Elsa drew back with her face going dead white again. "I believe you," she whispered. "I believe you were certain of yourself and what you would do. What kind of a man are you? What are you made of?" Her voice broke on the question.

Barry's face did not change. "I just happen to be a man who was trained to do a certain job. The years of training equipped me to meet easily such a minor crisis as I have encountered tonight."

He bowed to the girl and Moreland. "Please believe that I appreciate your offer of friendship. But I can have no friends. You have seen for yourself how quickly these enemies of mine are to strike at me through those whom they believe are my friends. I must be a man without friends. Until I find the man I seek I am a man with a cause only. Good night."

Moreland said harshly, "Chase, if you ever need financial help; if there is anything I can do for you, call upon me. You'll find me ready."

"I am sure I shall," Barry replied evenly. "But I hardly think I shall ever be forced to call upon anyone. I do not do things that way. Good night."

At the door Elsa turned back and stared at Barry for a moment. He stood as she had left him, gazing impassively at the men on the floor. Outside Joe had started the motor of the car. Barry lifted his head and smiled at the girl in the doorway. "Better hurry," he said. "Your car is waiting. I'll feel better when you are safely out of all this."

The girl's voice was still very low: "You're a hard man, Mr. Chase. In some ways you are not human. But deep down I think you are very human. Some day I shall see you again and prove that."

After she had gone, Barry knew that she was right. He was very human. It was his human grief and rage that had made him the killer in the dark. For he had seen, as he would always see upon this quest, the form of the gray man, lying on the steps. He would see the mild face of Carpenter a mask of blood. He would see always the pitiful remains of Bill Cleghorn.

All that was human, pitifully human. But behind that

humanness was the other man; the man that years of training had made; a man who was a relentless machine that
once set in motion would not stop until the end had come.
And that machine had been set in motion. He had been
graduated in red. His career had begun.

A WEEK LATER Archie Fonsdale moved into a commodi-
ous apartment in lower Manhattan. He stood in a window
gazing down at the green triangle of park. A few things
bothered him. But that worry did not show on his vacuous
face. His face looked strangely long and lax.

One of his troubles was Joe. He needed Joe, didn't intend
to get along without him. But the bronzed Indian would
be easy to spot. He would give Barry Chase away, would
lead his enemies to Gerald Sanderson. He wondered how
he would arrange for Joe. He would have to find a way.

A noise behind him made him turn. A dark man was
in the doorway, bowing, smiling broadly. His skin looked
brown and oily. He rubbed his hands softly and said, "Mlis-
ter Flonsdale, me number one boy. Fliend Joe hire me. Six
years one master San Francisco. Glood cook. Damn fline
boy, me."

His smile pulled his lips up at the corners, made a cres-
cent of guileless pleasure. His black eyes twinkled. His hair
was plastered close to his head. "By Jove," Archie Fonsdale
said, "that's ripping. Perfectly ripping! I suppose you know
where you sleep and what you have to do, and all that sort
of thing, eh? What's your name, boy?"

"Toyo. Know plenty about gentleman. Gleat pleasure
you leave everything to me."

For one brief instant Barry's eyes gleamed. Then they

became vacuous and empty as he turned toward the window. His smile was almost a simper.

He was thinking of what the gray man had told him, when he spoke of Carpenter's ability to become a different man. "Joe has a few tricks of disguise that are as good as Carpenter's."

He had forgotten that and he didn't like to forget anything. His life depended on how well he could remember. He must not forget again. But the thought of Joe staying beside him pleased him. He and Joe would start the hunt together. He gazed across the park at the serried skyline of buildings. Somewhere out there his enemy was hidden. He smiled, but the smile was vacant and silly.

6

THE LEGION OF PALADINS

LISTENING TO THE booming voice that beat over the radio on an evening two weeks later, Barry forgot for the moment his own mission. To be a free man he must find the man who had killed his father and mother. But the flowing eloquence of the voice that came from the loudspeaker touched something deeper than his desire for vengeance, or even freedom.

The voice of Anthony Carthage, booming forth his message to his Legion of Paladins, struck a deep and disquieting note in Barry's heart. And he knew that in millions of hearts across the continent that same voice was booming, building on the mounting spirit of unrest and fear that was sweeping the nation like a mighty wind.

As Archie Fonsdale, he had made the rounds of the night clubs and hot spots. Keyed to gather impressions, his keen senses alert, he had caught the undercurrent of fear that drove the throngs to seek escape in a mad fever of gaiety. And beyond the night clubs, Barry knew, was the growing army of Paladins who listened to the voice of Anthony Carthage and believed what he said: that America was being threatened; that the walls of order and reason

were being overthrown by the lawless element that week
by week was becoming bolder and more ruthless.

The two weeks he had spent in the city began to awaken
Barry to what he had dimly felt in the quietness of the hills.
His country was threatened. But underneath the fear and
disorder and lawlessness was something ominous, fearsome and hideous.

Anthony Carthage's voice filled the room.

"Paladins of America, be ready! I do not ask you to knit
yourself into an illegal army. We have learned our lesson
through the bitter experiences with our underworld armies.
But as men and citizens, hold yourselves in readiness. The
enemies of law and order, of Americanism and Christianity are in the ascendancy. My election of November the
fourth is already conceded. So certain it is that the millions
of voters will send me to the White House that the army
of darkness is aroused. Those who would trample under-
foot our dearest and most precious ideals know what will
happen when our party is in power. I tell you, Paladins of
America, they will strike before that day. Before that day
the same menacing powers which today make a mockery of
law and civilization will strike in the full strength of their
power. Therefore I say unto you, be Paladins! Be ready to
stand for all those things which your forefathers won for
you—Liberty!—Democracy!—Freedom!"

Barry turned his head and his gray eyes were brooding as they met Joe's level stare. For the moment Archie
Fonsdale was dead. Barry's voice was harsh. "What do you
make of it, Joe?"

Joe shook his head. "I only know that hell is brewing
somewhere. Sometime between now and election there

will be an explosion that will rock this old country of ours to its foundations. Someone is building up for that explosion."

"Carthage knows it," Barry said evenly. "He's building on it. The country knows it beyond shadow of a doubt. Crimes of violence increased ten-fold within the last two months. The police seem to be powerless. Banks are looted. Insurance companies by the score have gone bankrupt covering the losses in jewelry and valuables. And Carthage's stock leaps daily. What's the answer?"

"I figured up this morning," Joe said. "Twenty Paladin local meetings were broken up last week with a total of fifty fatalities and hundreds of lesser casualties. There's something big behind this."

"There's a local meeting of the Paladins uptown tonight," Barry remarked. "I'm going to attend. Better come along."

SO IT WAS that three hours later Barry stood on the fringe of the crowd that packed the vacant lot and listened to the dynamic eloquence of the man who stood on the platform under the white glare of the spotlight. His voice poured effortlessly from the mighty throat and huge chest. He had a mane of black hair that was swept back from his high forehead. His eyes were the eyes of a fanatic; his voice the voice of a rabble-rouser. A lieutenant super-demagog, Carthage.

Yet he preached no force. He cried for no massing of men in legions of fighting Paladins. But again and again he struck on the note of ominous foreboding. He urged the Paladins, as heroes of an America that trembled on the brink of destruction and chaos, to hold to the principles of liberty, democracy and freedom for which they, as Paladins, stood.

The temper of the crowd was easy to gauge. At each high point of eloquence the murmur that ran through it was like the growling of a great beast. There were no wild bursts of applause; no outbreaks of enthusiasm; just that ominous mutter of uneasiness and fear and resentment. To Barry it was more frightening and threatening than any outburst of fury or anger.

Joe was separated from him by a few yards. In glancing at him Barry saw the man at his elbow. His hard jaw was rigid. His eyes lifted to the speaker on the platform— burned with a light of something like speculation. There was intelligence in the fellow's face. And something else; something strong and straight and clean. Barry felt himself liking the fellow instantly. Their eyes met, and Barry felt as though they had spoken to each other without opening their mouths.

The huge crowd was restless. It surged in waves that seemed to push toward the platform and then ebb with the sway of their emotions. People jostled him, pushed him away. It was some little time before he realized that the jostling had suddenly become pointed and purposeful. He glanced at the man who stood beside him and suddenly understood why. The man was ringed by a half dozen others with "thug" stamped on their faces.

One of them spoke out of the side of his mouth, his words coming to Barry's ears as he found himself alertly listening. To anyone else it would have been an indistinguishable murmur. To Barry it was clear and understand-

*With the ease of a magician
taking a rabbit from a hat,
Brisson produced an automatic.*

able. "Just go along without any fuss and you'll live longer. Keep walking. One funny move and we'll plug you."

Barry caught a glimpse of the fellow's face, strained, imploring. It was as if he were trying to get some message across to Barry. And Barry looked at Joe and caught an understanding nod. He slipped along the edge of the crowd, unobtrusively, noiselessly.

Away from the crowd he paused as the thugs pushed their captive into a big sedan and crawled in after him. The motor roared and the car rolled away from the curb. Barry flagged a passing taxi and jumped in just as Joe reached him.

In the back seat Joe said, "Better not tail that car too closely. I spotted one of the hoods in the crowd that snatched that fellow. He's Shark Peters. He's one of Death Cardoza's mob. They hang out in a joint farther down town. It's a place with an undertaking parlor for a front. I'll bet money that's where they're taking this chap. You going to string along?"

"Yes, Joe, I'm going to string along. I don't know the fellow they snatched. But he's somebody of importance, I'll bet money on that. He was at that meeting for a reason. The thugs evidently knew it and picked him up. We'll see what we can do about it."

JOE FLASHED A grin in the dimness of the cab. "Swell! I was beginning to think I'd lose all of my Injun cunning if we went inactive much longer." He leaned over and touched the cabby on the shoulder. "Drop back a little, bud. We know where our friends are going."

The driver threw a glance over his shoulder and grunted an unintelligible response. It was to be seen that he didn't like trailing that black sedan. Cars like that had become more dangerous than ever they had been in the wild days of rum-running and highjacking. In fact, the present reign of gang terror made anything in the past seem pale and weak.

Barry leaned back in the car and murmured, "I leave it to you, Joe. Tell the driver when to stop." He closed his eyes and relaxed until Joe leaned forward and tapped the driver on the shoulder again.

He paid the cab and watched the red tail-light wink out of sight down the street, then followed Joe soundlessly. A few yards short of an angular building Joe put his mouth to Barry's ear and breathed: "That's the place ahead. There'll be a gangster at the door. They tell me it's a regular fort that nothing short of an artillery could crack."

Barry nodded. He touched Joe on the arm, their old sign of caution, and began to sidle along keeping to the shadows. His muscles trembled ecstatically as the old thrill ran along his nerves. He was a hunter again, playing the game that called for all caution and nerve and strength that years of training had drilled into him. But this time it was a real game. The men he faced were trained killers; killers who had grown more bold and ruthless than ever before as the power of the police failed to cope with the growing spirit of lawlessness and unrest.

There was, as Joe had said, a man at the door. He leaned one shoulder against the side of the door and watched the street. But there was no alertness in his poise. He stood there in the shadow of the building, like an indicative figure of crime, grown bold and at the same time negligent.

He never knew what hit him. Barry came out of the shadow in a tigerish leap that landed him on the man before he could open his mouth. His right struck the fellow's chin like a thunderbolt and he collapsed sound-lessly.

Barry tried the door tentatively. It was, as Joe had said, a miniature fort. The door was as solid as if it were a part of the wall. Without hesitation Barry dragged the gangster away from the building and dropped him to lay inertly in the darkness. From the holster under the thug's armpit he lifted the heavy automatic and crept back to the door.

Joe was standing in the shadows. "There was another out in the car," he whispered. "I fixed him so he won't bother us. Now, what do we do? How do we crack this pill box?"

Barry chuckled. "When stealth won't do, use boldness. You taught me that yourself, Joe. Now I use it." He lifted the gun muzzle of the gun toward the sky and blasted the silence with three shots.

Joe flattened himself against the building as the door

was flung wide and a stream of yellow light poured across the sidewalk. Barry slid down, both arms clutched around his stomach, his head on his chest.

The first man yelled out sharply, "What happened, Gus?"

His voice thick as though with agony, Barry sobbed, "They got me in the belly! Three of them! They ran across the street."

The man turned his head and yelled, "Come on, you guys! Someone plugged Gus and beat it."

He ran across the street with three men at his heels. Barry slammed the big door and shut them out, heard the yell of alarm.

Joe had slipped in beside him. A man ran from an inner room into the hall. He lifted his gun just as Joe's flung knife struck him in the throat.

Joe ran over and jerked the knife out as someone above yelled, "Hey, what the hell is going on down there?"

Barry jerked his head toward the back as Joe straightened. "Find the fuse box and kill the lights." As he said it the four men outside began to hammer on the door.

THE MAN ABOVE leaped downstairs three steps at a time. Flattened against the wall beside the stairway, Barry waited till the man had reached the bottom, then the butt of the automatic fell with a crushing force on the man's skull; the challenger fell forward on his face.

Barry stood listening for a second with no other sound from above. Behind him the thundering blows on the door were growing louder. Then, as he hesitated, a door opened above. Barry heard a strangled, gurgling yell of pain that made the short hairs on his neck bristle.

A man came to the head of the stairs and peered down.

Barry caught a glimpse of the man's face and felt his own face grow hard, his throat tighten. The head was absolutely hairless. The bald dome was high and bony. His forehead came down sharp like a protective armor to hang low over the deep-set, smoldering eyes. His mouth was wide, his lips as colorless as the putty-colored cheeks that were stretched so tightly over the structure of his face that his cheekbones seemed to be coming through the skin. This was the infamous Death Cardoza, merciless killer, one of the petty rulers in the empire of crime.

Then like an enveloping blanket darkness fell. Barry heard Cardoza whirl and start back along the corridor. Barry raced up the stairs. As Cardoza whirled the gun in his hand slashed the darkness with lances of flame. Barry felt the hot wind of death on his cheek. A slug tugged at his coat sleeve. He threw a slug in return and heard Cardoza's gasp of pain and knew he had made a hit.

He reached the door just as Cardoza flung it shut behind him. Barry threw it back, leaped into the room and spun sideways. His back against the wall, he squatted on his heels and listened. Across the room a man was breathing in deep, sobbing breaths. The agony in the gasps made Barry's skin prickle and the muscles along his jaw tighten.

There were three other men in the room. Barry located them by their motions. He smiled thinly. They probably believed they were keeping silent. They couldn't know that to Barry's ears they gave themselves away by a thousand signs. Two of them wore watches. The ticking beat on his ears through the thunder on the lower door that did not cease. One of them moved and his shoes squeaked.

Frozen into immobility, his breath light and shallow,

Barry spotted them. The man who was breathing in such agony was undoubtedly the man the thugs had picked up at the mass meeting of the Paladins. One of the others would be Death Cardoza, the other two a pair of henchmen.

Barry knew when Joe reached the doorway. But to the other men in the room his coming was as soundless as the flow of calm water. They did not know he was there till his knife glittered in the dim light that filtered through one dirt-caked window. And one of the men didn't even know that. For his yell of astonishment ended in a gurgling gasp.

The man who had been sobbing brokenly seemed to be recovering. His breath was more even and controlled. From afar came the wail of sirens. The gunfire had drawn the attention of the police. Barry heard the rasp of clothing against a coarser material and knew then that Cardoza and his remaining henchmen had fled. The thundering tumult at the door below had ceased with the first screams of the police sirens.

Joe's whisper was loud in the quiet room. "Cardoza had a getaway door. I'll find it and see where it leads if you'll look after the fellow they snatched."

The man in the chair was bound. Barry cut the bonds. One of the man's arms was twisted out of shape. He shivered as Barry touched him and said with an attempt at jocularity, "You'll have to handle with care. I guess I'm kind of shop-worn."

7

THE FAT MAN

JOE CAME BACK into the room as the man shakily stood on his feet. Joe said harshly, "Cardoza made a getaway. He left the punk at the end of the passage to get us coming down. I took care of him. The cops are coming now. Are we going to wait for them?"

Barry started to shake his head in negation as the stranger said hoarsely, "No. Let's get out of this. I don't want to get held up by the police. I'll tell you about it as we go along."

Following Joe down the narrow passage that led down a steep flight of steps, Barry had the man's good arm over his shoulder, half-carrying him since his wabbling legs seemed unequal to the task of holding him up.

At the bottom of the steps the fellow gripped Barry's shoulder weakly and said, "I got to take a chance on you, whoever you are. You must be all right or you wouldn't have followed up and got me loose. I can't see myself getting away in the shape I'm in." His voice went thicker and weaker. "I'm all busted up inside. They kicked a few ribs in bringing me here. If anything happens to me go to Washington and see General Jeffery. Tell him K59 sent you.

Sewn in the cuff of my trousers you'll find a slip of paper. Take that to General Jeffery."

Barry snapped, "All right, I'll do that. But right now I'm going to see if I can't get you out of this. Joe! Where does this passage lead?"

"It comes out in an old tenement basement next door. That's where Cardoza left his man. If I'm not mistaken Cardoza went for reinforcements. We'd better hurry if we want to get this boy out of this mess."

As they emerged from the dark passage into the musty basement Barry froze. There were other men in the basement with them. He jerked his gun loose just as a flashlight cut a dazzling path through the dusty dark. Guns roared. Barry felt the man at his side jerk with the impact of a slug as he fired, instinctively shattering the flashlight with his first shot. Beside him Joe's gun roared twice. Slugs whanged viciously into the cement wall. One whined by his ear as he dropped. His own gun spoke twice.

Rolling over, he came close to the man he had rescued. He was breathing hoarsely. His voice came gaspingly: "Got me! Do your stuff, buddy! See the chief. I—" He gasped, shuddered and went limp.

Cold rage ran like an icy torrent through Barry. The man he had come to help was dead.

There were other men there in the dark. Cardoza had evidently collected the men who had been hammering at the door. Crouching motionless there in the dark, Barry spotted them. There were four of them. One would be Cardoza. Barry's voice was as thin as a knife edge as he whispered: "You're finished, Cardoza. I'm going to kill you. You're going to die as a rat should—in the dark, squalling."

The answer was the roar of a gun across the basement. But Barry was ten feet away when the gun spoke. He drove a slug into the streak of gunfire and heard the man gasp as the bullet found its mark. Farther along the wall Joe fired twice.

In the silence that dropped on the heels of the gunfire Barry took stock. There were only two men alive against them in the darkness. Barry listened. One of the men, he felt certain, was Cardoza. Both of them were getting jittery. Their jerky breathing and uneasy stirrings showed that. Barry's whisper went on relentlessly, throwing panic into the men who faced him.

"I'm coming after you, Cardoza! I could plug you now. But I won't. I'm going to kill you with my hands. I'm going to give you some of the stuff you handed out to the fellow you picked up at the mass meeting. I don't think you can take it, Cardoza."

HE HEARD THE rasp of leather on cement and threw a slug in that direction. He cursed softly as he heard the whine of the glancing bullet.

"There's a pillar of some kind between us and the stairs that Cardoza and his pal just used," Joe said softly. "We'll have to wait for another day to pay our little score with Cardoza." He chuckled harshly. "For a guy with no scalp lock, he was damned scared of an Indian."

Barry rolled the dead man over and ran through his pockets. As he expected they were empty. Cardoza and his men would have seen to that. His questing fingers found the thing he sought, a little cylinder of thin paper sewn in the cuff of the trousers. He slipped it into his pocket and said as he straightened up: "Let's move, Joe. We're in up to our necks in the biggest game we've ever tackled."

In the apartment he kept under the name of Archie Fonsdale, Barry said: "We started on a quest of our own, Joe. I vote now that we forget it for the moment. There's something bigger to do. The land beneath our feet is in flames, or I'm a rotten guesser."

Joe's bronze face was emotionless. But his black eyes were alive with a light that was hard and sharp. "I've got an Injun hunch," he said, "that when we get to the core of this mystery we're going to be very damn close to the man we want."

He paused. "Twenty years ago this man was smart enough to fool the best of the police. He controlled crime. He has controlled it since. He must be a megalo-maniac now. Mere control of crime wouldn't satisfy a man like that forever. He must be getting along in years. My guess is that he's got a deep plan floated now. It's all tied up with the army of thugs that have suddenly all but paralyzed law and order. And there's a reason behind it all, a damned deep and tremendous reason."

Barry nodded. "I was thinking along the same lines myself. But my first job calls for a trip to Washington. I'll start immediately."

"We'll have to move softly, Barry. Every thug in New York will be looking for us now."

"I'm going alone," Barry corrected. "You stay here, Joe. Keep on working for a lead. I will find it easier reaching Washington alone than I would with you. You're the one who has to worry. You've got to stay here where the real threat is."

"I knew you'd say that," Joe said regretfully. "It's the smart thing to do." He came around the table and laid his hand briefly on Barry's shoulder. "Hop to it, youngster! Do your stuff. I'll be pulling for you."

The buzz of the doorbell brought them both alertly around. Joe dropped back into character. "Toyo go slee who come," he said and shuffled to the door.

Over Joe's shoulder Barry studied the man at the door. He had never seen anyone quite like him before. He was short and fat and dumpy. His voice was a cheery treble. "I wished to see Mr. Archie Fonsdale." His gaze went past Joe to rest on Barry and he smiled cherubically.

Barry said, "You may show him in, Toyo."

Something stirred warningly in Barry's breast as the little man came in. He was dressed in a bright blue suit with a yellow shirt and dark blue necktie. The gloves he held in one dimpled hand were gray-blue. His moon face writhed in a perpetual smile. His blue eyes were sharp and clear as a summer sky. His lips were full and very red. His hair under the gray hat was startlingly red.

AS JOE STARTED to back out of the room the little man said, "No, Joe, I want you to stay. I want to talk to both of you." He smiled benignly, brushed a fleck of dust from his lapel and then had a big automatic in his hand. He had pulled it with the ease of a magician taking a rabbit from a hat.

"We have been very interested in you boys," he said in his high treble. "Oh, my goodness, yes; very interested. It took us quite some time to learn that Archie Fonsdale was Gerald Sanderson, better known as Barry Chase. But we did find out, you see." He chuckled, his round little paunch shaking as though he were thoroughly enjoying his little joke.

"You see," he went on cheerfully, the snout of the big gun as steady as a rock in his dimpled hand, "when you played with those rough boys you came home too directly."

He sighed. "Really, our Mr. Cardoza, while very efficient at times, is hardly up to par mentally. At times like this I find it distinctly necessary to act myself."

He shook his head and his red lips pursed in mock petulance. "But dear me, I enjoy it. I must admit that I do enjoy it. Especially when I have to deal with two such charming fellows as yourselves. Although," he added with a glance at the windows through which the sunlight streamed, "I chose an inopportune time for you. I believe, my dear fellows, that you prefer to work your hocus pocus in the dark."

"Your monologue," Barry said evenly, "while entertaining to a degree, is merely that. Would you kindly, since you seem to have the situation so well in hand, explain the nature of your visit?"

"Why, certainly, gentlemen, certainly!" He shook all over with mirth. "I've come to kill you both, gentlemen." He shook the snout of the gun at Joe and said playfully, "Tut! Tut! Mustn't make any untoward moves, my friend, or your span of life will be cut still shorter. You see," he explained, "I am so much more dangerous than our fearsome friend Mr. Cardoza. I could shoot you, friend Joe, while you were reaching for that very handy knife of yours. I could follow that, my dear Mr. Sanderson, as efficient as you are with a gun, by shooting you before you cleared that gun from the holster under your arm."

Barry smiled and bowed. "I am always ready to admit when I meet one who holds the winning cards. But standing up is tiresome. Won't you sit down? And perhaps allow me to do the same?"

As he sat down in the big chair, very carefully keeping his hands in sight, Barry felt his nerves tighten. This little fat man was no braggart. He was more dangerous than a dozen Cardozas rolled into one. His bright blue eyes were the eyes of a killer, a killer who would strike while he smiled, without warning or change of expression. The way he backed to the chair and sat down without relaxing a whit of his vigilance proved that. Barry knew that he was facing now one of the real leaders in the mystery that threatened America.

The little man leaned forward in the chair and said gently: "There is the matter of a trifling paper you abstracted from the zealous young man who was killed last night. I would like to have that paper."

Barry bowed. "Would you, really? Now that does complicate things, doesn't it?" As he talked he was as alert as a panther who crouches by a water hole waiting for his prey. The little man's eyes told him nothing. The sounds from the outer hall did. But he kept talking. "If you kill us it may be difficult to locate the much-wanted document."

THE LITTLE MAN shook his head. "Dear me, gentlemen, you do under-estimate me! I said I came to kill you. I did. But you may choose a quick and comparatively easy end or what, I assure you, will be most unpleasantly lingering and prolonged." As he spoke Barry saw for an instant behind the mask of bland humor a cruelty and savagery that was ruthless and terrible.

Keeping his hands on his knees, Barry pulled his feet back and leaned forward, "My chubby little friend," he said easily, "this conversation becomes tiresome. Why not bring our little comedy to an end and talk business? Like this!"

As he spoke he jabbed his heel on the button beside his chair leg. The chair in which the fat man sat tipped backward, catapulting the little man over its back. His gun exploded, sending a slug ripping into the plaster of the ceiling.

The gun under Barry's armpit leaped into his hand. In a single stride he was standing over the fat man, who dropped the gun as he gazed up into the cold blaze of Barry's eyes.

"You have one stupidity in common with your hench-men," Barry said quietly. "You will persist in under-esti-mating your opponent. I never make that mistake. Because of that I installed the trick chair for just such an emer-gency."

He saw the quick glance the little man threw toward the door and smiled gently. "Joe and I have been listening to your friends in the hall for some time. There again you under-estimated. I wonder, my chubby and cheery friend, how you happened to have lived so long with such mental handicaps as you possess." Without turning his head he snapped, "All right, Joe, let them in!"

With his gun jabbed into the fat man's back, he swung him around to stand as a shield between him and the door. Joe jerked the door open with his left hand. The big auto-matic in his other hand rose and fell once as the man stum-bled into the room. Beyond the door a second man swung his gun with a jerk and pulled the trigger. Flattened against the wall, Joe snapped a shot that doubled the gangster up. Then the intruder collapsed slowly, his two hands clutching at his chest.

Joe closed the door slowly. "There were only two," he said tonelessly. "I heard them come up after the fat boy."

The little man had recovered his composure. He carefully brushed the back of his trousers where they had touched the floor. He started to brush his lapels when Barry caught his wrist and jerked him around. Joe moved automatically. His hands ran up and down the little man. He tossed out a tiny pistol and a long-bladed knife.

"Gentlemen," the visitor chuckled, "you embarrass me." Then his blue eyes glittered. "You also made me appear very clumsy. That I cannot forgive. Some day I shall have the pleasure of killing you both for that."

"The trouble with you, chubby," Barry said casually, "is that you have developed a slight touch of insanity as a result of your association with your very mad boss. You will never kill me. To prove that, I am going to let you go to report to your boss. I'm afraid that he'll be more than a little angry. You have bungled badly. Not only have you failed to kill me but you have also wiped out the character of Archie Fonsdale without knowing what part I shall play next."

Joe said harshly: "The cops will be here any minute." He jerked his head toward the door, behind which rose a babble of shrill excitement. He threw a glance toward the window. "If you'll take my advice you'll drop that fat slug down ten stories to the street. It may be quite a while before we get such a chance again."

Barry shook his head. "No, Joe; I want this pleasant little chap to report back to his boss. I have ideas."

"You have never had a worse one than that," the fat man said imperturbably. "It will probably cost you your life before many days."

Barry bowed. "I'll take that chance. Now, since the police may be here asking awkward questions before long, may I bid you a very warm adieu? I know we shall meet again. I shall look forward to that meeting with pleasure."

The little man clicked his heels as he bowed deeply. "The pleasure of that meeting will be all mine," he said suavely. "By the way, I am known to my friends as Brisson. Some of them fancifully and playfully refer to me as the Red Terror. I am sure that I shall live up to my reputation where you are concerned."

As the door closed behind the little man, Barry slipped the automatic back under his armpit and whirled. "Come on, Joe, down the back way. Toyo and Archie Fonsdale are dead."

8

ROLY-POLY DYNAMITE

HE PAUSED FOR an instant as someone began to hammer on the door. He heard the fat man's treble lifted in the hall: "I was calling on Mr. Fonsdale when these two men broke in on us."

Barry didn't wait to hear more. The police were trying to smash the door down now. Whirling, he followed Joe down the back stairs toward the alley entrance.

Barry caught a glimpse of a uniformed copper at the end of the alley as they came out of the entrance. Across the alley was the entrance to another building. As the policeman at the alley's mouth turned to gaze up the street the two of them dashed across the passage and went through the open door. They walked through the building and came out on the open street in time to signal a passing cab and roll away from the section.

Joe said dryly: "Well, that's that! Now the cops will be looking for Barry Chase, alias Archie Fondsdale. Just another handicap, Barry. They'll be hunting for a Jap boy or an Indian or both as well. This game is getting red hot."

"And it will be hotter," Barry said evenly. "Our little fat friend will never quit now until he catches up with us. He'll throw the whole weight of his organization into the hunt for us. Evading the police will be child's play compared to the job of keeping ahead of Brisson."

"I still think," Joe insisted, "that you made a mistake in not heaving him out the window."

Shaking his head, Barry said slowly: "No, Joe, I don't think it was a mistake. Brisson is a bloodhound. He'll stick to our trail now till he or we happen to die. But he's the main road to the man at the top. That little fat fop is one of the key men in the organization. Sooner or later he'll lead us to the man we want."

"If I don't kill him first," Joe said thinly. "Just as sure as hell, Barry, he'll either kill us or force us to kill him. The next chance I get I'm going to do a job on him. He's had one break. He won't get another."

In the downtown retreat, Barry talked to Joe while he fitted himself into another character. "While I'm making my move to Washington try to find out more about Brisson. Get everything you can on him. Find out where he fits. But watch your step."

Joe grinned. "You're telling me. Brother, I don't underestimate that roly-poly stick of dynamite. But you are the one to worry. Brisson will guess you're heading for Washington. He'll move earth and hell to stop you. He was making a bold, desperate move when he came here. He'll be more desperate than ever after what happened today. And, at the same time, he'll be more cautious. You watch your step, buddy, and don't worry about me."

Barry knew Joe was right. Brisson was clever and dangerous. He would be doubly dangerous now because of his temporary failure. Dressed in the cheap suit that was part of his character, he tried to look ahead and plan his steps, and knew that he would just have to take things as they came and watch for the breaks.

Walking through the Pennsylvania Station he studied the people about him. Here, as everywhere else, the same feeling of nervous tension prevailed. The station was crowded. Most of the people, Barry shrewdly figured, were men and women who were able to leave the city and go back to the country that seemed safer than this hell-hole of fear and tension that the city had become.

His own disguise, he believed, was good enough. The suit he wore was ill-fitting. It went with the cheap paper suitcase in his hand. The shoddy hat was part of the costume. So, too, was the vacant, wide-eyed stare with which he watched his fellow travelers. There must be no failure.

HE HAD LEFT Joe in the apartment downtown. Leaving there he had traveled for an hour on the subway, watching the people around him in an attempt to find out if he were still being shadowed, giving Joe time to arrange his act in this play. He could afford to take no chances. Every train, bus and plane to Washington would be watched by men who would not be afraid to strike at any time and anywhere. He wondered how clever Brisson was at penetrating a disguise.

He stopped wondering in the concourse of the station and stiffened with a jerk at the prod of the gun in his ribs. Brisson's treble voice bubbled gleefully.

"Well, well, if it isn't my dear friend Gerald! Dear boy, you should never wear such obvious disguises. Although I must admit you do it very well. You almost had me fooled for a minute. And I pride myself on my ability to penetrate a disguise instantly."

There was a mocking light dancing in the bright blue eyes. Behind that was something cold and deadly and watchful. Barry knew that this time Brisson would take no chances. He would kill without compunction or warning.

The man with him was huge, raw-boned. He had pale eyes in a wide, flat face. Those eyes were fixed as unwaveringly on Barry as were Brisson's.

Barry let no trace of his tension show on his immobile face.

Brisson chuckled and his paunch joggled. "I figured that you would go the obvious way, but in disguise. My dear fellow, you never should have tried to outwit me."

Barry watched the red-cap sauntering across the rotunda, then let his eyes come back to meet Brisson's stare. He smiled gently. "My fat and amusing friend, outwitting you is child's play. You saw through the disguise. Did you imagine I would come without a second trick up my sleeve? Or do you insist on sticking your head into a noose by continuing to underestimate me? Think about it, Brisson! Think about it, my chubby little rascal!"

The red-cap reached them and thrust out a hand toward Barry's suitcase. "Carry yuh bag, suh?" he asked solicitously.

The flat-faced man snarled, "No!" and pushed the red-cap away.

Brisson's eyes gleamed as his hand went under his lapel. His lips flattened as he snapped, "That damned Indian! I should have known!"

The gun in Joe's hand came down in a terrific chopping stroke that laid Brisson's forehead open in a long gash. He went back, both arms out-flung, to land on his back.

The big man jerked around to meet the jab of Joe's

muzzle. Barry felt the snout of the gun that had menaced him through the cloth of the man's coat relax.

He grinned at Joe. "Nice work. Take him for a walk while I get out of this."

Two or three people had halted and stared in swift amazement at what they must have thought was a fight. A woman stared at the prone figure of Brisson, saw the blood streaming from his forehead, screamed and fainted. The crowd had pushed in with a babble of excitement. Now it surged back.

Somewhere in the crowd Joe was walking swiftly with the big man. Barry whirled and walked, in the opposite direction. More people came running. He saw the glint of metal buttons. In another minute the police would be bending over Brisson, listening to a dozen different versions of what had happened.

ONE OF THE things that had been drilled in Barry over the years was a knowledge of crowd psychology. He knew that not one around him at the moment of Joe's attack would be able to swear as to who hit whom, or how.

Outside the station he threw himself into a taxi and snapped a downtown address at the driver. When they reached lower Sixth Avenue, Barry leaned forward and said, "I've changed my mind. Drive straight on through the Holland Tunnel to Newark."

At Newark he paid off his curious driver and found another who would drive him to Philadelphia. At Philadelphia he would catch a train.

He felt more secure now. Brisson had penetrated his disguise. But it would be quite some time before Brisson would be able to give coherent orders. Joe had struck with vicious strength, probably praying that it would kill the little fat man. But Barry knew that the blow hadn't been enough. Brisson would be after them. But not until he got patched up and was rid of his headache. Barry figured he had enough leeway to reach Washington.

He caught a train at Philadelphia and rode unmolested to Washington. As he rode he was thinking of the man who had been tortured and killed, of the little man who looked like a jolly elf, and was more dangerous than any man Barry had ever known. He was thinking of a voice that rolled sonorously from loud speakers all over the nation; a voice that had some connection with the trouble that seethed beneath the surface.

In the big office to which he was directed in Washington, a keen-eyed clerk whisked him through a railing into an inner office when he mentioned K59.

Inside the office two men went over him meticulously. One of them removed the gun from under his arm. They found the tiny automatic strapped to the leg just above the ankle. They found the knife that he carried between his shoulder blades. They found everything but the sliver of steel he carried in the back of his belt. Which pleased Barry. That was one weapon that no one ever seemed to spot.

When he was disarmed a big-shouldered man came into the room with quick, nervous strides. Under his black eyebrows his eyes were hard and probing. "Sorry if you're not all right, but we can take no chances. There are those who might try to crash the gate and take a pot shot at the Chief. You say you have a message from K59?"

Barry nodded. "A message from K59 to General Jeffery.

I was told to deliver to no one but General Jeffery. You are not General Jeffery."

For a full half-minute the big man stared at Barry with inscrutable eyes. "I am Colonel Varden," he said brusquely, "chief aide to General Jeffery. You may tell me what you have to report to General Jeffery."

"Sorry," Barry said tersely, "but my message was for General Jeffery, not his chief aide."

A shadow of something like admiration crossed the hard eyes. "I'm glad you know how to keep your mouth shut. I guess what you have is really important. Follow me."

THE MAN BEHIND the wide desk in the big office raised his head. His hair was as white as snow, his eyes as clear and bright and hard as icicles. But his voice was very mild as he asked, "What is it, Colonel Varden?"

"This man claims to have a message from K59 which he refuses to deliver to anyone but you."

General Jeffery stood up swiftly and leaned across the desk. His thin hands trembled as he leaned on them and stared at Barry. "K59! Where is K59? Why didn't he come himself?"

"K59," Barry said harshly, "was killed last night. He was tortured first by a man named Cardoza who tried to get information from him. We got him out of that but Cardoza shot him before he could get clear. Before he died he told me to come to you and give you this."

General Jeffery let the slip of paper rest on the desk while he continued to stare at Barry. "Who are you?" he asked.

Briefly Barry told his story. As he listened General

Jeffery sat down slowly. When Barry was through he
smiled gently.

"Yes, I remember now. The papers made a great play of
your adventure in Irontown. They played you up as some
sort of super-man. Frederick Moreland, whom you doubtless remember, said you were not underrated. I had been
wondering what had become of you until this morning."
The smile widened. "This morning, papers gave your name
another spread."

Barry glanced at the headlines. There had been no time
during the hectic day for a reading of the news. Now he saw
he was being sought in connection with a gang killing in
the Bronx. His lips twitched as he said, "There'll be more
in the evening papers, I imagine."

General Jeffery's thin eyebrows raised as he unfolded
the paper sent by K59 and said with a rising inflection,
"So? How is that?"

At the mention of Brisson's name General Jeffery
frowned. Colonel Varden said harshly, "Why didn't you
kill him when you had a chance? Brisson, boy, is one of
the most dangerous men in the country if not in the world.
You'd have given this Department its best news in months
if you'd brought the news of his death."

Glancing up from the thin sheet of paper before him,
General Jeffery asked harshly, "Have you any idea of what
this contains, Chase?"

Barry shook his head. "No, sir. I saw it was in code. K59
had no time to do more than tell me to bring it back to
you."

General Jeffery handed it to the Colonel and fixed Barry
with his hard stare. "Mr. Chase," he said. "I'm going to ask

you an unusual question. We don't do things this way often in this Department. But the times are unusual. Will you join us as an operative?"

Colonel Varden threw one swift glance from the paper he was reading to Barry, then went back to his study again. General Jeffery went on: "We have lost fifty men in the last year, Chase. Those fifty men represent the cream of our operatives. No one knows what happens to them. We did find one or two of them bullet-riddled. The rest have vanished as completely as if the earth had swallowed them. We are fighting now the worst menace that the nation has ever faced. And we are being forced to do it with green men."

He nodded at the slip Colonel Varden was reading. "K59 was one of the best. He was the cleverest and bravest of the lot. That's why he lived as long as he did. Now he is dead. We can chalk that up to Brisson. I think, when all is known, Brisson will get the credit for most of the killings.

"I am asking you to join us because you are the first man I know of who has met Brisson face to face twice and beaten him both times. I doubt if we have a man left who could have done that. Will you try it again?"

"I promised Brisson," Barry said evenly, "that I would meet him again and kill him."

9

NATIONAL CRISIS

JEFFERY'S THIN BROWS drew together, then relaxed as he smiled. "Good! I'll go over the whole thing with you now and show you what we're up against. I am giving away no state secrets. The whole country knows what is going on."

He took the slip of paper back from Colonel Varden and stared at it while he talked. "A year ago we became alarmed in this office at the increase in organized crime. Hitherto most of such organizations specialized in racketeering and extortion. This group began to pull huge-scale ventures. Big banks were looted. Prominent citizens were kidnaped and held for tremendous ransoms. Of course they collected tremendous sums of marked money. But for months none of that marked money appeared.

"We investigated. And almost as though our investigation was a signal the whole world of crime boiled over. Police were shot down wholesale. Our men were killed. And with the resultant break-down the marked money appeared. It showed up simultaneously in a dozen different places. We could trace none of it to any known source.

"It was at this time that the political organization known as the Legion of Paladins was formed. Groups of men began to join these so-called protective associations. Then Carthage came on the scene. Before that time Carthage had been a petty demagog of the usual tub-thumping variety. When he started to form the Legion of Paladins he showed uncanny organization ability and a more than uncanny knowledge of the crime situation and the temper of the people."

General Jeffery stared at Barry. And Barry knew that the General was waiting for him to make a comment. "So you believe that the rise of the Paladins was planned and fostered by the crime wave. You believe that this crime wave was staged to do exactly what it is doing, break up the morale of the police departments and shake the public confidence in their guardians."

The gleam in General Jeffery's eyes showed Barry that he had scored a bull's-eye. General Jeffery went on: "All that is needed in the present situation is a spark to light the tinder." He waved a thin hand toward the paper. "K59 thinks that the conflagration is planned. He tells us that the date for it is set as October Fourth. That means we have two weeks in which to uncover the plot and stop it taking place. You have shown us that you can be a valuable man."

Barry smiled. "Two valuable men, then, General Jeffery. If you get me you take Joe also."

Jeffery smiled. "Yes, Moreland told me about Joe also."

"You spoke of Moreland before. What part does he play in this game?"

"Moreland," Jeffery explained, "is the chairman of a group of influential business and professional men in New York who have thrown their resources into the fight for law and order. Why do you ask?"

Barry shrugged. "I know nothing of the man except that he told me he was a friend of my father. You know my part in the rescue of his niece."

Colonel Varden pushed a chair toward Barry. "Sit down. We might as well give you a picture of what you are up against since you're going on our staff."

FOR TWO HOURS Barry listened. The plot sounded like the fantastic outline of a nightmare. Yet it was held together and made plausible by an imagination and genius of planning that was like nothing the Government had ever run into before.

Secret Service agents sent out to run down angles never returned. Police forces were powerless. In some cities they were so demoralized that they made only a pretense at law enforcement. Murders by the hundreds were going unsolved. In most cases there was no real attempt at solution. The toll of organized crime during the two previous months ran into the hundreds of millions. And now the Paladins of Carthage were beginning to cause the authorities new headaches. For the Legion represented potentialities they hated to admit. If it were to clash with criminals as they were now organized to do, there would result something like a small civil war.

"We haven't got a thing on Carthage," General Jeffery said in answer to Barry's question. "But we know there must be a link with the forces who are bringing about disorder. If it were not for those forces, Carthage's Paladins never would have assumed political importance.

"Carthage has been careful to preach only organization and peaceful organization at that. He knows how to avoid the pitfalls run into by the Ku Kluxers and the Black

Legion. His men are welded into an organization to fight everything inimical to America. But he has organized. If, as K59 reports, a coup is planned for October Fourth, Carthage could then call upon his Paladins to throw their organization into the field and take over the job that police and militia had failed to do. We would then have, in effect and in power, Carthage as a dictator, backed by his millions of Paladins."

"You think he would then arm his Legion?" Barry asked quietly.

"We don't think. We know," Colonel Varden said harshly. "One of our agents sent us a message in code reporting the discovery of a cache of millions of machine guns, pistols and grenades. He was on his way in with further details when he disappeared."

Two hours later General Jeffery said, "I'd like you to stay and have dinner with the Colonel and myself. Once you leave here you will have little opportunity to see us again until this thing is broken."

General Jeffery smiled wearily. "You see I am a virtual prisoner in my suite of offices. I dare not go out on the street because of the constant danger of assassination. So I eat, sleep and work here."

While they ate, the evening papers were brought in. Barry glanced through them but found no account of the incident in the Pennsylvania Station. Brisson was evidently very much alive and was not pressing any charges against the man who had struck him down.

They were lingering over coffee when a clerk brought in a sheaf of papers and laid them down before General Jeffery. Jeffery glanced at them and his thin face hardened.

He shoved the papers across the table to Colonel Varden, saying harshly: "Another move! Read that, then tune in on Carthage's daily broadcast. He's due to speak in fifteen minutes. If I'm any guesser he'll have something to say about this; something that will be of tremendous importance to all of us."

Colonel Varden handed the papers to Barry as he finished reading. Barry felt his nerves tingle as he read. Five Paladin meetings in various cities had been broken up simultaneously by the use of gas. The police had been unprepared and powerless to act as carloads of gangsters rode in upon the meetings, flung their gas bombs and drove away. According to the reports thousands of Paladins were now in hospitals. All across the nation the Legion of Paladins were massing as they waited for some word from their national commander, Carthage.

WHEN THE BROADCAST began, Carthage's resonant voice filled the office with rolling echoes. General Jeffery leaned forward, his arms resting on the desk, his thin face set in lines of hard intensity. Colonel Varden stood behind him, legs spread, hands behind his back, head tipped back, his deep-set eyes glowing.

Barry lay back in his chair, perfectly relaxed, nerves and muscles at ease. Yet he knew in his heart that what he was now hearing was another chapter in the dramatic mystery that was piling up toward something new in America. Behind Brisson, and the unknown boss behind Carthage and his Legion of Paladins, a wave of terror and disaster was piling up. Should it reach its crest it would engulf the nation in a deluge of death and disaster.

"Paladins of America," the booming voice said, "you

have seen today the enemies of your country. They have struck openly and hideously. But do not allow yourselves at this moment any thoughts of vengeance. Some of your comrades have died. Thousands of them at this moment are gasping their lives out in the agony of suffocation. The enemies of law and order, of Christianity, of freedom and Democracy have come out into the open. But do not strike back. I implore you to hold yourselves like men.

"You are powerful, Paladins of America. In your millions you could wipe the nation free of the rats that infest it. In your might and unity you could rid this America we love of the pestilence that stalks in the darkness of crime and disorder. But, because you are so mighty, so irresistible in your strength and unity, you must be patient. You must make no move that would now label you as other than you are, the champions of justice—Paladins who may, when the final hours come, rear up a bulwark of strength between the enemy and those principles of liberty and justice for which you stand."

General Jeffery's comment was thin and reedy. "Clever! Do you see what he is leading up to, Varden?"

Varden nodded.

Carthage's voice boomed on: "But I do not ask you to stand defenseless before an enemy that is as bold as it is ruthless. I do not ask you Paladins to go meekly to your deaths in the wave of poison gas with which the enemy is flooding you. As you must keep your hearts and spirits clean and strong and unyielding, so must you protect yourself against the devastations of the devil who would destroy you.

"You represent a mighty army, Paladins of America; an

army dedicated to peace and order. Do not strike back. Give the authorities no opportunity to declare that you are an army that only waits to strike. But you must be protected. No one is stupid enough to deny you that right after what has happened tonight.

"I have seen this coming, Paladins of America. I have watched the terror of the enemy mounting toward some such outburst as we have witnessed this evening. And I have prepared for this emergency. Tonight as I speak to you from my watchtower, supplies of gas masks are on their way to every city, town and village in the United States. Every Paladin will receive a protective mask. Keep them with you wherever you go. Be on the alert. If gas is used against you again, wear these masks. But do not strike back. I command you to stand steadfast. Be ready. But also be firm. You constitute the hope of America, Paladins.

"Should the hour strike when the enemy casts off the last shred of caution and strikes openly, then you will be ready to defend the sacred rights of free citizens in a free and glorious America. This is your duty, Paladins! Stand ready to do your duty!"

"THE STAGE IS set," Jeffery said harshly as the resonant voice ceased. "Carthage is as clever as Satan himself. He does not make a statement that could be questioned. He is able to lay all the blame on the organized bands of criminals who break up his meetings and kill his men. Yet tonight from coast to coast a few million Paladins are seething with white rage. Carthage can hold them back for a while. But the time will come when he cannot hold them back longer."

"And the time isn't far in the future," Colonel Varden

growled. "He has taken the first step tonight. If the other wing strikes now, a few hundred thousand helpless people will die. The Paladins will be safe. Then, the rage that now consumes them will break forth irresistibly. Carthage won't be able to hold them back then. I can see them taking over all the duties of police and army. They will bring order out of chaos. By that time they will be armed and efficient. And Carthage will be Dictator of America."

"It is a plot almost without flaws," Barry said slowly. "If the outbreak comes and the Paladins restore order, then Carthage will be a national hero. The Paladins will be looked upon as saviors of their country. And they will be so powerful that no one can dictate to them—if they are allowed to arm."

"That," General Jeffery snapped, "is our big job now. Find out where these arms are concentrated. Find out when they are to be issued. Find out—if we can—what the coup is that is planned for October Fourth. If we don't uncover that and squelch it we might as well prepare to run for our lives. America as such will be a nation under the fist of a dictator."

"We should be hearing from Moreland," Varden said slowly. "His group of business men were making a survey of all possible plants and factories which might be making the armaments for Carthage's Legion. A week ago he reported the discovery of valuable leads and promised more information before the week was out."

"One by one our sources of information fail us," Jeffery said wearily. "Our best men disappear just when they approach the core of the mystery. Our Secret Service is only a shadow of what it was. We sit here at Headquarters helpless, tied hand and foot by a national enemy that is cleverer than anything we have ever faced in our history. We send out our agents and might just as well pass a sentence of death before we send them out. It has reached the point where an assignment is tantamount to a sentence of death to the man who gets it."

He fixed his cold eyes on Barry. "Are you willing to take on the job under the circumstances? I haven't tried to kid you. I've given it to you straight. We have had men in this service whom I trusted and admired. Looking at some of them a year ago I would have said that they would be able to handle any situation; that among them they could squelch any plot that might be concocted. One by one I have received reports of their deaths. I have watched my organization melt away until today we are next door to helplessness. Are you still ready to enlist?"

"I told you," Barry said evenly, "That I promised Brisson to face him again. I promised him that I would kill him. Somewhere above Brisson is some one with more vision and imagination even than that little fat genius. Through Brisson I get to that man. General Jeffery, you couldn't call me off now."

He went on: "I'll take the job. But I'll work my own way, use my own methods. I'll get Brisson. And through him I'll reach the number one man of this unholy alliance. By the way, are you sure that it is not Carthage who is boss of both wings?"

JEFFERY SHOOK HIS head. "We're sure of that. We know Carthage's record. He's a born demagog. He can sway a crowd as no other man in America can. But up till the present he has been just that. He lacks the brains and the ability necessary to concoct such a scheme as this.

"That applies also to Brisson. The man is a cold-hearted scheming devil. He has a brain that is unexcelled in carrying out orders and fooling his opponents. But he hasn't, no more than has Carthage, the genius to plan anything on the scale that this plot is staged. This, my boy, is the biggest plot ever concocted on this old planet of ours."

"But there is one man at the head of it," Barry said musingly. "That's the one inherent weakness. Catch that man, disclose his link with organized gangland on one hand and Carthage on the other, and you shatter the whole thing. The Legion of Paladins will automatically dissolve into disorganized rabbles that can be handled by the police and army."

"Yes," Colonel Varden said ironically, "that's all we have to do, my boy. All we have to do is put our finger on a man who has evaded us for twenty years."

Barry nodded calmly. "There's just one thing in our favor. In the past this unknown could hide himself more readily. Today he is nearer the surface than perhaps we imagine. His coup is ready to spring. He must naturally be in close touch with his various leaders. The critical juncture of affairs demands that. Therefore I have a better chance than any one man you have ever assigned to the job before."

"But they know you now," Jeffery said slowly. "Every agent they have will be on the lookout for you."

"I have proven that my disguises will fool all of them but Brisson. That little man has an uncanny ability to see through disguises. Therefore, I shall go ahead and make plans to outguess him when we meet again. I did it before.

I foresaw the possibility of a surprise in my apartment and set my trap with the collapsible chair. I foresaw that he would attempt to head me off at Pennsylvania Station and had Joe ready to play his hand. I shall do the same thing again."

But even as he spoke, Barry knew that Brisson would be harder to fool the next time. He had twice made the mistake of under-rating his opponent. He would not make that mistake a third time.

"I have been waiting two days for a report from Moreland," Jeffery said crisply. "For some reason it hasn't come. And it is of the utmost importance now. Moreland was attempting, with the help of several reputable financial and business leaders, to form a business bureau that would operate to help us. Moreland was chairman of the group. Over a period of weeks he reported the functioning of the group. They hired investigators to supplement our staff. Last week he sent a secret report telling us that one of his men had uncovered something that seemed to lead directly to the core of the plot. Since then we haven't heard a word. Your first job will be to get in touch with Moreland and find out why his report has been delayed. Get leads from him and get to work at the point to which his investigator has progressed."

All three men turned as the clerk entered the office with a slip of paper in his hand. Barry, staring at the man's gravity, knew that he bore more bad news. He watched Jeffery's face harden as he read the paper.

Jeffery's gaze traveled from Colonel Varden to Barry as he said: "This is to report that Moreland and his niece, Elsa Barrow, have been kidnaped! They disappeared from their home yesterday without a trace. There has been no demand for ransom. Which means, probably, that no ransom will be demanded. Moreland knew too much and so was removed."

Barry felt himself go cold inside. He thought of Elsa Barrow. Her disappearance could mean but one thing. The men behind this plot would have no compunction about killing her. Indeed, nothing else could happen. People who knew too much were dealt with summarily in this game.

10

FEAR RAMPANT

GENERAL JEFFERY'S VOICE was harsh. "That changes your orders, Chase. Now, if Moreland is alive, find him. But I doubt that he is. These fiends take no chances. Find Brisson again. If you can beat him again you may find your way to the man at the center. Once we spot him we can break the whole mystery wide open. If we don't the whole nation will be in danger. Find Brisson and the man behind him."

He began to pace the room soundlessly. "We must find out what is to happen on October Fourth. We must forestall the event whatever it is. If we can do that we can show Carthage up and ruin his chances of election." He smiled faintly. "A sizeable assignment, young man. I know all about your strange education. It seems it was done for a bigger and more important reason than anyone ever imagined. Go out and put your training to good use."

SLOUCHED ON A park bench, a battered hat pulled down over his eyes, hands deep in the pockets of his ragged coat, Barry watched the thin stream of pedestrians as they hurried through the park. All were marked with the same stamp of nervous fear. Their white faces mirrored the fact that terror had frayed their nerves and shaken their hearts. A nation of men and women went about their tasks in a disorganized world with the spectre of disaster hounding them.

Barry did not turn his head as the ragged Negro slumped at the other end of the bench. But his trained ears picked up every word of the talk that did not reach beyond the bench.

"I worked on the guy who was with Brisson at the station," Joe mumbled. "He didn't know much. Just a strong-armed guy employed by Brisson. One of the kind who are never told much. He only knew one thing. October Fourth is tied up with Baxter City."

Baxter City, Barry knew, was a big steel and manufacturing center. Named after Jeff Baxter, the steel king, who had first located his plants there, it had grown like a mushroom over a period of years. Automobile plants had moved in. A city of factories turning out everything from auto parts to locomotives sprawled around the steel mills. Anything could happen in Baxter City.

He was talking about the fat, redheaded man. "Brisson?" he whispered.

"They took him to a hospital. Soon as he was patched up he disappeared." His sigh was a sibilant hiss. "I wish to hell I had been able to hit harder. Maybe I should have plugged him. I should have taken my chance and shot him through the heart."

Barry shook his head. "We want Brisson alive for a little while. He can lead us to the boss who stands behind him."

Joe went on: "Before I got through with the big guy he told me that Carthage is going to make a personal appearance at a mass meeting of Paladins in Baxter City, Thursday night. There are a few hundred thousand Paladins among the workers there. There's dynamite behind that meeting."

"Any hint of what happened to Moreland and his niece?"

Joe flicked his fingers outward. "Gone just like that. No fuss. No leads. Just vanished. One thing more, Brisson has a hangout in a joint on Charter Street."

Barry slumped further back in his seat. "Keep digging. I'll tail you when you leave here to see if anyone has spotted you. We'll meet at the old hangout down town. Plan on getting to Baxter City by Thursday."

He watched Joe slouch away. Hands still deep in his pockets, shoulders slumped, hat low over his unshaved face, Barry followed. He watched Joe cross the street.

An old woman came out of the shadows of the building. She was short and fat. The shapeless rag of a dress she wore made her look fatter. Something in her walk made Barry withdraw into the shadows of a bush at the park entrance.

Joe crossed under the street light and slouched along the street. The fat woman followed. Barry could hear her wheezy panting as she wabbled along. Then his nerves tightened. Behind the frowzy mask of her appearance walked Brisson. And he had spotted Joe.

In the shadow of the bush, Barry watched, suddenly tense and alert. He saw Joe whirl to meet the man who stepped from the darkened doorway. Joe's hand was under his armpit when another stepped in fast and crashed a blackjack on Joe's head.

At that exact instant a sedan shot down the street and swerved into the curb. A door swung open and the two men tossed Joe inside. Brisson waddled across the sidewalk and jumped into the car with the two men and the sedan shot up the street.

It was all done so swiftly that Barry had no time to move. The two or three pedestrians in the street hardly glanced at the swift surge of action. Innocent bystanders took no chances on noticing too much these days. The only reward for curiosity was a bullet through the brain or a knife in the back.

Barry watched the car take a left turn and figured that the driver was heading downtown. Somewhere near Charter Street, Brisson had a hangout. Barry crossed the street in rapid strides. As he walked, he watched for a taxi. He had to find Brisson's hangout and get Joe out of the hands of the killers. A cold finger of dread ran along his spine. He knew what faced Joe. They would torture him and attempt to get information from him. And knowing Joe, he knew that the Indian would take stoically all they could hand out. He would allow himself to be torn to shreds but he wouldn't talk. Somehow Barry had to get on the job before they went to work on Joe.

11

CONTACT

BEFORE HE WENT to Charter Street, Barry slouched into a bar on Third Avenue. The three men along the bar looked like a deputation of panhandlers. Barry stood at the elbow of a tall man with a patch over one eye. He leaned over the bar, gaunt shoulders stooped, one hand clutching a whiskey glass.

He turned and glared at Barry out of his one good eye, an eye that carried the malevolence that twisted the thin lips into a perpetual snarl. His nose had been broken at one time, thickened and pushed sideways.

Barry said, "Beer!" to the moon-faced bartender and snapped a quarter on the bar. The coin bounced twice. Barry's hand slapped down on it at the end of the second bounce. Beside him he felt the big man stiffen. But the snarling lips did not change expression. The good eye still glared at him.

When his change came Barry pushed the dime back to the bartender. "Gimme two nickels," he snapped. "I wanna do some telephoning."

He drank the beer and walked out of the saloon, tossing the nickel in the air, letting it clink back into his hand with the other two. He did not glance again at the three men at the bar.

Around the corner he slipped into the doorway of a tenement and sat down on the steps. A drunk came in, stumbled over Barry and kicked at him with a snarling outburst of profanity, stumbled up the stairs, fumbled with the knob and went in.

Barry continued to wait. He heard the clock on the corner toll eleven. He waited ten minutes more before the man with the patch on his eye came in and walked by him. Without a word Barry got up and followed the man, through a redolent hallway, up a flight of rickety stairs into a shabby room.

The one-eyed man snapped the switch of a single dusty bulb, stared at Barry with his one glittering eye and said, "Well?"

"The chief told me how to contact you," Barry said. "I'm taking K59's place. He said to say, 'Big Jeff sent me'."

The one-eyed man snapped, "What happened to K59, and where do you come in on the deal?"

Briefly, Barry told him of K59's death and his trip to Washington. The one-eyed man swore in a savage monotone. "So they got him. Death Cardoza, eh? That's another reason for my killing that corpse-faced sadist." Then the gleam in his single eye sharpened. "What have you on now?"

Just as briefly Barry told him of contacting Joe and of what had happened. The one-eyed man broke in again. "Brisson! You expect to outsmart that fox?"

Barry shook his head. "He's not so smart. He was tailing Joe. But he didn't see him contact me. That was a bad slip

*The fat man swung the gun and
said, "Come right in, Buddy."*

on his part. Now we're going to outsmart him again. We've
got to. Joe is my friend. That would be reason enough for
my wanting to rescue him. But more important is the fact
that we can't afford to lose Joe at this stage of the game.
He's too valuable to lose."

The big man nodded. "Okay, brother, I'm your man. This
is your game. So give your orders and let's get started."

AS BARRY OUTLINED his plan the one-eyed man smiled
sardonically. "It sounds simple enough. But I happen to
know about that joint on Charter Street. You can't get
within a block of it without Brisson knowing."

Barry smiled gently. "Brisson will figure that I will be
on his trail. He'll have a trap set for me. I can imagine just
about what it will be. He'll pull in his men and allow me
to reach his hideout. When we do you'll carry out your
orders. I'll give you more instructions after I go over the
whole layout thoroughly."

Barry left the one-eyed man several blocks away from

Charter Street, with orders to follow later. Alone he prowled through the alley that backed the tenement that K40, the one-eyed operative, had described. He crouched at the back for ten minutes, as motionless and silent as part of the wall. At the end of ten minutes he heard the stir of the man who waited inside.

Coming to his feet, he inched soundlessly along the wall till he stood just clear of the doorway. He held a blackjack aloft with his right hand; with his left he tossed the handful of pebbles he carried, one by one into the alley just beyond the door. He smiled mirthlessly as the man inside cautiously thrust his head outward, eyes and ears straining.

The blackjack came down with crushing force on the back of the head. Then Barry's left hand caught the man's collar and stopped him from falling. He carried him away from the building and laid him gently against the far wall. The man was dead.

Inside the musty cellar Barry moved with the same caution. He found the meter board and went over it inch by inch. For fifteen minutes he worked over the cellar. Returning soundlessly to the door, he found the one-eyed man waiting.

With his mouth to the fellow's ear he gave him whispered instructions.

"Remember, time your move precisely. Too soon or too late will be fatal to our plans. I know Brisson. He will spend just so much time in gloating. That's his one great weakness. He is as clever as Satan. But he knows it too well. He'll want to rub the fact of his cleverness in on me."

"Go to it, big boy," the one-eyed man said softly. "I hope you've got it doped out right. I sure hope you have."

"I have," Barry said calmly. "Keep your gun ready. They'll come after you. Take no chances with them."

The one-eyed man chuckled thinly. "As if you had to tell me that!"

Back in the alley Barry traveled away from the house. He came back into the street and walked boldly along the block to the front door. As he expected, no one was there. He climbed the short flight of steps into the narrow hallway and halted in the darkness, muscles and nerves relaxed.

He had not long to wait. Lights came on to shine with dizzying brilliance. A voice snarled, "Up with them, smart guy!"

Doors on either side of the hallway stood open. In each was a man with a Tommy gun. Barry turned slowly and gazed up the stairs as a reedy voice piped: "So we meet again, Mr. Chase! This time, I assure you, the pleasure is mine." The voice snapped: "Regan, come up behind him and strip him of his guns. Be sure to get the one he carries strapped just above his ankle. It's sure to be there. All these clever young hunters carry a spare."

Regan's voice was harsh with wonder. "He ain't heeled, Boss. There's no gun on him."

BRISSON'S VOICE BECAME more edged. "All right, Chase. Come up the stairs slowly. Very slowly and carefully. One quick move and my men will mow you down."

Barry followed the reedy voice into the room beyond. It was a big room, with a flat-topped desk at one end. Over at one side Joe was roped to a chair. His bronze face was puffed and swollen. One eye was closed. The other one seemed to be trying to warn Barry of something.

Back of Joe's chair stood Death Cardoza. One arm was

in a sling. His eyes were lambent with the dancing flame of hatred. On either side of Cardoza stood men with ready automatics.

Brisson went over and sat down behind the desk. The patch of adhesive on his forehead was new and white. Behind him two men leaned against the wall and watched Barry, their guns trained on him.

"I perceive," Barry said calmly, "that I was expected. You honor me by the thoroughness of your preparation."

Brisson's red lips curved in a cherubic smile.

"The preparations are so much more thorough than you could imagine, Mr. Chase. You are a most droll young man, you know. Your training, I fear, has in itself been a limitation. Your little plans for throwing the enemy into darkness are, to say the least, amusing. This time, I warn you, I have prepared for you. This time the man you so thoughtfully placed in the basement to cut the lights will not help you very much."

As Brisson talked, Barry saw the new shining light fixtures with their dead bulbs. He met Joe's imploring stare and smiled.

Brisson's gaze darted from Joe to Barry. "What your henchman is trying to tell you, my entertaining young Galahad, is that you have been outwitted this time. You have walked into the trap I set for you. To be perfectly frank, I must admit that you have surprised me. Several things about your entry surprised me."

He paused. "You know, I almost hoped that you would fail to walk into the trap. It irks me to have you fall so far short of my estimate of you. I would much rather you had tried some more unorthodox method of approach. It would have given spice to our little game. You pain me, young man; indeed you do!"

Death Cardoza's voice was a thick croak: "Is all this hot air necessary, Brisson? Why not get to work on the guy and get it over with? You promised to let me—"

Brisson laughed gleefully. "Don't let your bloodthirsty desires run away with you, Cardoza." Then his chubby face suddenly tautened. All the humor flowed out of it, leaving it flat and hard; as hard as the bright blue eyes. "Besides, Cardoza, I am not accustomed to having my orders questioned. You do what you are told at the appointed time. Do not be so bold as to question those orders unless you have lost your desire to continue living."

CARDOZA'S EYES MIRRORED his stark fear of the stout man. His lips tightened. "I didn't mean it that way, boss," he said hoarsely. "It was just that I wanted a chance to go to work on the guy."

"A very laudible ambition," Brisson said with humor flowing back into his face again. "It does you credit, Cardoza. And I must admit I look forward to the treat as much as you do."

He licked his red lips with a little pointed tongue.

With a trained sixth sense Barry was checking off the seconds. The man in the basement would act on clocklike schedule. His gaze traveled calmly from Brisson around the room, over the faces of the four gunmen. It lingered briefly and coldly on Death Cardoza's cold eyes and twisted lips, and came at last to Joe's face.

"Now, my young friend," Brisson said, with the same mirth dancing in his voice, "since the time approaches for you to make your daring spectacular move, I must disenchant you. You are very clever in many ways. In others, as I pointed out before, past success and the nature of your training have combined to limit you. The man in the basement will soon cut the lights. Then what do you think will happen?"

Brisson chuckled and went on. "Not the swift sally in the dark, my crusader. Oh, no, not that! I expected that and prepared accordingly. Instead, something altogether different will happen."

He paused and licked his lips again. Barry could see that the pudgy sadist was gloating over his coming triumph. "Instead of that, my dear young friend, there will be more light than ever. When the lights go out I turn on more. See?" He pointed to the switch.

"Knowing that you would come," he chuckled, "I simply had a secondary line run in. When the lights go out, I throw my switch and bring light back to the darkened scene. You should never have attempted to cross wits with me, my callow friend."

Barry let no trace of emotion appear in his face or voice. Brisson, staring at him, laughed a little, but this time there was a trace of nervousness.

Barry's voice was icy, biting in its contempt. "I told you before on two occasions what I now tell you again, Brisson. You are rather a fat and contemptible fool. You have brains of a sort. But you have had so much success in outwitting others that it has gone to your head. For the third time, Brisson, you have, underestimated me. I wonder how many more times you can do it and live?"

Brisson's face froze into a mask of hard savagery. Cardoza's breath was suddenly loud and panting in the silence.

Joe leaned forward. He was ready to move. By his pose Barry knew that he had cut the bonds on his hands. The gunmen against the walls were suddenly like cats, ready to pounce at the first move.

Brisson put a dimpled hand on the desk. Barry felt his throat grow dry and tight. The time was not yet. If Brisson acted now all was lost. He must stop him, stall him some way.

Barry leaned forward. "I am going to kill you, Brisson. I am going to kill you soon, if someone else does not beat me to the job. I am not boasting, Brisson. I leave that to fat fools like yourself. I am merely stating a fact. I am going to kill you."

Brisson's red lips curved into a smile again. "A very brave bluff, my young cockerel. You crow rather loudly and forcefully. But this time I have you. Watch! When I throw this switch, watch those dead bulbs come to life. The cellar is fixed in the same manner. When your henchman cuts the line I throw this switch. Then the cellar too will be lighted, giving my men opportunity to kill your helper. Clever, isn't it?"

Barry watched Brisson's fat hand creep to the switch. On Brisson's face was a smirk of self-satisfaction.

"Remember," Barry said slowly, "I warned you, Brisson, You've made the same mistake again."

Brisson said: "Watch the lights come on when I throw the switch. I do not believe I shall wait for your deluded helper to cut the line."

He threw the switch on his desk with a convulsive motion of his hand. The auxiliary bulbs stayed gray and dead.

12

IMP OF SATAN

BARRY SAW CARDOZA jerk the gun from under his arm, saw the gunmen lean forward, gun-muzzles steadying, saw Brisson's mouth open to shout as the lights went out.

With the blink of the lights, Barry drew the knife from the scabbard between his shoulders and flipped it, all in one single motion before he ducked low and leaped.

One of the gunmen behind Joe screamed shrilly, horribly, then went down across an empty chair that had overturned with a crash. That empty chair, Barry knew, was the one that held Joe a split-second before.

Where Cardoza had stood, a gun boomed in a muffled report. It was as if the one who had pulled the trigger held it close to a body as he fired.

Barry whirled silently back toward Brisson's desk. He heard the breath of the nearer gunman. One hand caught the gun and whirled the man around. The other came across and down in the killing blow struck with the side of the hand. The gunman sobbed once and collapsed.

Barry stood in the darkness, balancing in his hand the gun he had taken from the gangster. Someone touched him lightly. Joe's whisper was almost soundless, yet it vibrated with exultation: "I got Cardoza. I'll swing back and take the fellow who is still across the room. Get Brisson."

Squatted on his heels, Barry said in a whisper that was as dry and sharp as the rustle of winter wind in dead grass: "I told you, Brisson! I warned you, you fat fool. How many more times do you expect to meet me and remain alive?"

The man beside Brisson fingered the trigger with jittery nervousness, blasting the darkness with flashes of his gun. Barry triggered the automatic just once after the third flash and heard the man's grunt as the slug struck him.

Across the room there was a sodden thud of metal on cushioned bone and the flop of a body on the floor. From far below came the dull boom of gunfire as the one-eyed man fought it out with the two men who had been placed to get him. But it would be the two men who would be overcome with surprise. Listening tensely, Barry heard Joe across the room open the door and slide out into the hall.

"Joe has gone after your henchmen below, Brisson," Barry whispered. "They won't have a chance. No more chance, Brisson, than you have with me now."

He was trying to prod Brisson into movement. Trying to get him to shoot so that he could locate him in the darkness. But the little fat man was frozen there somewhere, not daring to make a move or sound.

Barry's voice went on relentlessly: "I knew you would take the precaution of running another line. I knew how your clever brain would work. So I searched until I found the line, then cut it. You should have thought of that Brisson. You would have thought of it if you hadn't been so proud. You are not very clever, Brisson. Not clever enough to get away with your little game much longer. You're going to die tonight, Brisson. You're going to die here in the dark."

HE PAUSED AND listened. A machine gun below lifted its voice in a hysterical chatter. Barry thought of that night when other machine guns had chattered under the quiet stars and his best friends had died to their chant. Then an automatic boomed once, hollowly, flatly, and the voice of the machine gun died abruptly.

"Number one of your machine gunners," Barry went on relentlessly. "If number two and Regan don't break away and run like rabbits they'll follow number one."

Biting scorn edged Barry's voice. "You must be very proud of your peerless organization, Brisson. You must be consumed with pride at your magnificent organization that can be crossed up and torn to ribbons by those at whom you so lately sneered."

Brisson's desk made a tremendous crash as it went over. Barry felt a touch of admiration for the little fat man who, even when his game went against him, could still recover and think quickly.

Brisson's gun blasted again and again. But Barry made no attempt to shoot back. Brisson was covered by the top of the desk. And Barry guessed that it was made thick and solid for just such an emergency. Instead of returning the fire, he circled the room noiselessly, smiling as he watched the lances of flame.

When the gun clicked on an empty shell, Barry laughed harshly. "Now what, Brisson? I'll tell you. It's death now, my fat friend!"

"Oh, no," Brisson said sharply. "But it will be for you

shortly. Crow over your little victory. It will be short-lived. I'll see you in the morgue."

Barry leaped across the room. Behind the overturned desk a trap-door slammed hollowly. Cursing, Barry searched for it in the darkness. He had been guilty of a grave error that time. He should have known that the wily little crook would not have allowed himself to be cornered where there was no way out in case of failure.

He found the trap door and swung it wide. In the room below he heard a quick scurry of motion and the bang of another door. He started to leap through but withdrew slowly instead. Brisson was gone. There was no question of that. The present move must be away from this place before Brisson could surround it with his gangsters.

Halting for a second, Barry listened. One of the men on the floor groaned hollowly. From the others there was no sound. He thought of crossing to make sure of Cardoza. But Joe had said he had finished Cardoza. Joe wouldn't have said that if he wasn't sure.

Barry slipped out into the corridor and halted. Below, the second machine gun suddenly filled the building with hammering thunder. In the dim light that filtered through from the street Barry could see Joe taking cover behind a newel post at the foot of the stairs. Joe's gun roared once. Somewhere below, the machine gun crashed to the floor. The gunner coughed and took three stamping strides forward, then fell.

Without turning his head Joe said, "Regan beat it. We'd better get out of this before the gangsters start swarming back."

Someone moved at the far end of the corridor and

brought them whirling alertly around. Then a harsh whisper said: "K40. Don't plug me."

HE CAME FORWARD, his one good eye gleaming, his hard face cracked in a grin. "I spotted you between me and the door. I cut down two guys in the cellar. They popped out just as you said when I cut the lights. I take it they were considerably amazed when their lights didn't come on as they expected."

Joe jerked around toward Barry. "Brisson! Did you get Brisson?"

"No, Joe, he got away. He had a trap door behind the desk."

Joe cursed in a savage monotone. "The fat devil! He sat there chuckling while they kicked me around. I didn't mind that. He was sure his extra line would work the trick. I thought it would myself."

Barry said tersely: "You and Bill trained me better than that, Joe. But never mind that now. We pulled our job. Let's get out of this. Brisson will keep for another time."

"Another time," Joe said hoarsely. "So help me, Barry, I'll take him first another time. I'll take him first if I have to jump over a dozen others. All I ask is one more chance."

As they went through the alley toward another street the one-eyed man chuckled. "I like the way you boys play. I've been here in New York taking it on the chin from these rats so long it began to get under my skin. You fellows have the right idea. I wish I could stick with you."

They stood silently in the street listening to the wail of police sirens entering Charter Street. The one-eyed man chuckled grimly. "They waited till they were sure the shooting was all over before they barged in. Being a cop these days is being in a tough racket."

"They can't help it," Barry said softly. "But one of these days, I've got a hunch that the old siren will mean what it once did. Get this thing under control and I'm willing to wager that our police forces will be twice as effective as they ever were. They've been learning plenty this past year."

"I only hope," Joe said dryly, "that their period of training doesn't have to last much longer."

"Or that they don't have to hand over their job to the Paladins," Barry added sharply. "That would be the worst ending possible."

Later, in the room of the one-eyed man, who told Barry his name was Grant Page, the talk switched back to the Paladins and the mass meeting which was to be addressed by Anthony Carthage in person.

"The Chief gave me a free hand," Barry told the others. "I'm to try to get a line on Moreland. Brisson could tell us where Moreland is. But catching Brisson now won't be so easy."

"He'll be almost certain to be at Baxter City if the action is centering there now," Grant said thoughtfully. "Everything points to Carthage as the storm center now. Anything that breaks will only push him and his Paladins further into the limelight. Whatever happens will be staged for the express purpose of allowing him to make logical moves in assembling and arming his Paladins."

"Exactly what I was thinking," Barry said. "If Brisson is going to be at Baxter City that's where I'm going to be also."

"Do I go along?" Grant asked eagerly. "Or do I stick

around here chasing shadows the way I've been doing the past two months?"

Barry smiled. "The Chief had a hunch that you were rather stalemated on your job here. If I could use you in any capacity, he told me, I was to do so. If you want to throw in with us on the Baxter City front I don't see why you shouldn't do it. You can't do much here in the city now."

GRANT BANGED THE table with a big fist. "Great! Now, maybe I'll see some action. Maybe I'll get a crack at Brisson."

He stared at his big hands as he opened and closed them slowly. His voice was thick and slow. "I just want to get these two hands on his fat throat. I'd rather do that than throw a slug into him. I want him to feel the life being choked out of him."

Barry felt a shiver run over him as he met the glare of the one eye and the savage twist of the big mouth. He had been trained to recognize killers and he knew Brisson would get swift justice from the one-eyed man.

"There was a kid on the job with me last month. He was just out of college, fired with the idea that he was doing a great work for his country in the time of need. He was a swell kid. He was full of pep and fire. And on top of that he was clean and young and eager." Grant let his chin rest on his chest as he talked. "Brisson caught up with him. He tried to make the kid talk. Next morning Brisson tossed what was left of him in the park."

He raised his head and stared at Joe. "You say you plugged Cardoza tonight. I wish I'd had that privilege. Cardoza was Brisson's prize torturer. I have an idea he did the work on the kid. But Brisson is worse than Cardoza. Brisson stands back while Cardoza works, and chuckles."

"Yes," Joe said softly. "I got Cardoza. I yanked his own gun out of his hands and stuck it into his ribs when I pulled the trigger."

Joe's face was a bronze mask. "Sometimes," he said slowly, "I get the feeling that I want to revert to type. You say Brisson will know where Moreland is being held? I'd like to get Brisson staked down a little while. I'd make him talk."

"Brisson knows if anybody does," Barry said. "You may get your chance yet, Joe."

13

THE BIG SLOB

THEY DECIDED TO scatter, to go separately to Baxter City.

"We have a headquarters there," said Grant. "A cheap lodging house on Power House Street, down in the slums. We have an operative there. A fellow by the name of John Webster. He's a big slob, with a pair of watery, sleepy eyes and a moon face, but he is worth more than a half dozen guys in a pinch.

"John will put us wise to the ropes. The house number is 256. We can split now and meet there."

"But watch your step," Barry warned. "I know you will, of course. But remember, every instant Brisson will be expecting us. He will figure on our arriving in force because of Carthage's personal appearance. He'll be planning on making a roundup of our men who are covering the event. Remember and walk accordingly."

Grant Page stood up, his good eye gleaming. He gripped Barry's hand and said harshly, "So long, buddy. Good hunting. I'll be with you in Baxter City if I'm still alive. You can bank on that. And I'm going to try like hell to stay alive until I've choked that little fat crook to death."

Gripping Barry's hand, he said in a strained whisper, "I omitted to mention the boy Brisson tortured was my kid brother. Maybe you can guess how I feel. That's why I want Brisson if it is humanly possible. I ask that chance if it turns up."

"I guess," Barry said slowly, "that under the circumstances you get it. Brisson is yours." He stared for a long time into the one gleaming eye. "If I knew that a fellow like you were on my tail I might get panicky."

Grant shook Joe's hand and sauntered to the door. He lifted his hand in salute and said, "See you on the battlefield." The door closed softly behind him and his feet made muffled sounds on the rickety stairs.

"There," said Joe softly, "went one swell guy. We should be able to raise a nice brand of hell with Brisson in Baxter City."

Barry was thinking of a slim girl with a glory of bronze hair and fine eyes that looked squarely at you. That girl was in Brisson's hands now. He wondered briefly if he'd give Grant his chance at Brisson if anything happened to Elsa.

As though reading his thoughts, Joe leaned across the table and said, "Forget it, Barry. The girl is alive or she isn't alive. Thinking about it won't help. Remember what Bill would say."

Barry said, "Yes, I'll remember."

Joe said shortly: "Let's go. I'll slip out first. Give me a few minutes' start and you can head for Baxter City as directly as you wish. I won't be more than a couple of jumps behind you."

The door opened and closed noiselessly. Listening, Barry could not hear a sound from the stairway. Even on those rickety stairs Joe moved as soundlessly as the drift of smoke.

Barry waited for five minutes, then as noiselessly as Joe, drifted out of the house and into the street. A splatter of chill rain blew into his face. An elevated train thundered off into the distance headed uptown. Had his nerves been trained to a lesser degree Barry would have shivered. For he thought of men like Brisson and Carthage with their gangs of outlaws, tearing the fabric of law and order to shreds that they might control the destinies of a nation. The rumble of the elevated was like an echo of impending disaster. The Paladins in Baxter City might rumble into action like that under the leadership of Anthony Carthage.

BAXTER CITY WAS a city of whispers. As Barry slouched along the street, dressed in greasy overalls, khaki shirt open at the throat, a threadbare coat and a battered felt hat, he looked like the man he was supposed to be, a steel worker or mechanic looking for work. But as he went his cold gray eyes took in everything. His keen ears were alert to the whispers that circulated.

In the bars, men gathered in rows and talked in blurred undertones. They stood in little groups on street corners and around the entrances to buildings and talked in whispers. And, while they talked, their eyes were searching, scrutinizing everyone who came near them. These men were at the breaking point. They waited only the touch of a spark to set off an explosion of rage and resentment.

And in twenty-four hours Anthony Carthage would come before them to harangue them. Anything could come out of the meeting.

All the men he saw were workers. Nowhere did he see the faces of the thugs of the type that served under Brisson. If these men were in town, and they must be, they

were under cover, hiding for whatever stroke their boss
had planned.

NUMBER 256 POWER HOUSE STREET was a ramshackle
building in a street that looked as if it were in the last
stages of dilapidation. The street took its name from the
big, grimy power plant on the corner. There were a few
dingy stores, a slovenly bar. For the rest, the disconsolate
houses frowned into the filthy shabbiness.

Listening after he knocked, Barry heard someone walking heavily down the corridor. Loose and worn boards
creaked complainingly under the heavy tread that was as
slow and heavy as a cow's.

Barry was prepared for a fat man. But expecting an operative who had the reputation of being one of the best, he
hardly expected what he saw. A huge, beefy face with a
coarse stubble of dirty brown beard. Under the stubble,
skin the color of old suet. Eyes like stale oysters.

The man stared at Barry for several seconds. Then his
voice came in a husky croak out of the barrel chest. "Yeah.
Whatta yuh want?"

Even as General Jeffery had told him how to contact
Grant, so Grant had told him how to approach John
Webster. "I'm looking for a room," Barry said softly. He
paused. "A very special kind of a room."

The expressionless eyes did not change. "So yuh want a
very special kind of a room."

"Yes," Barry went on, "I want a room with special furni-
ture. The kind that don't squeal."

The man in the doorway nodded heavily. "I suppose,"
he croaked, "you want special windows in the room, too."

"Sure," Barry said, "the kind that only look one way. Big Jeff said you'd have such a room."

The big man backed up ponderously. "I guess I've got what you want," he said heavily. "Come on in."

The stairs creaked as if on the point of collapse as the big man climbed laboriously. He went down the hall, opened a door and waited for Barry to come into the room.

He said: "I don't know you. You're a new fixture. When did you come into the game?"

Barry rapidly ran over his entry into the service. As he talked John nodded weightily. He sat in a chair that he engulfed beneath his bulk. He folded a pair of hands like hams across his big paunch and stared at Barry like a sour-visaged Buddha. When Barry had finished, he said heavily: "I heard about it. It came through the grapevine. Anyone else with you?"

At the mention of Grant Page's name, the leaden eyes seemed to grow bright and sharp for an instant. "It's time some of you came! Hell is ready to pop. So far I've been getting away with murder. But sometimes I have a feeling there's a gun at the back of my neck."

He said it as though he were making a remark about the weather. "What do you think of tomorrow night?"

Barry shook his head. "We can only guess. I thought you might be able to tell us something."

The heavy mouth pursed. "Nobody knows anything. The guys at the top of the local Paladins don't know a damned thing. They only guess that something big is piling up. My guess is that no one outside of a few who are putting on the show know what's behind it."

THE SHRUG OF his shoulders was like the slow heave of

a hippo surging out of the mud. "One guess is as good as another. Baxter City is center of steel. It's center of automobiles. It's center of the arms industry. It would make a hell of a fine distribution point for armored cars, and bombs. If the Paladins took over the town, Carthage could get a hell of a lot of stuff moved in a hurry. It's my guess it's ready to move. There's been a lot of rumors of arms and armored cars being manufactured for foreign shipment. Nothing has been moved abroad though. All of it is still in Baxter City."

He closed his eyes, giving the impression of infinite weariness. "One or two of the boys found out things. Those boys are dead now."

"No idea as to the identity of the big boss?" Barry knew the question was foolish when he asked it.

"You think I'd be sitting around here if I knew?" John rumbled contemptuously. "No one knows who the big boss is. I doubt if anyone outside of Brisson and Carthage know it. And they won't tell. Not unless we could get them where we could persuade them."

"That's your job," John continued heavily. "I'm no good at that sort of thing any longer. All I can do is to keep my mouth shut and my ears open."

He closed his eyes again. When he opened them Barry got the impression of an agony of regret. "I'd like to see some action once more. But I'm getting older and fatter every day." He stared through the dirty window. "Maybe," he said, with some deep and inner hope lightening his voice, "I'll get a chance yet. I might get some action now."

He turned slowly, the chair creaking as he turned. His huge body seemed to move very deliberately. But even as he turned he had a big gun in his hand. He swung the muzzle and said. "Come right in, buddy."

14

HIDE-OUT

JOE CAME IN. He threw a thin smile at Barry and said, "I saw you come in. I thought I'd play safe in case you'd gotten off on the wrong foot. So I slipped in the back way."

"Didn't the cook notice you?"

Joe smiled. "I slipped by when she wasn't looking."

"You must be a damned ghost," he rumbled. "Nothing but a ghost could get by Sarah. That's why I hang onto her."

In the street a man began to sing drunkenly. The gun in John's hand disappeared as magically as it had appeared. He rose, the chair groaning again as though in relief. "That's one of my damned roomers," he rumbled. "Coming in drunk as early as this. A hell of a state things are coming to."

The drunk came in the front door and stumbled up the stairs. In the doorway he suddenly went cold sober. His one good eye gleamed. "Hiyah, boys. All present and in one piece, I see. Great going!"

John said: "Grant, you old son of a slob, I'm glad to see you." The opaque film lifted from his eyes and dropped again like a shutter. That was the expression that accompanied the words. But Barry noticed the way the huge paw gripped Grant's hand.

"Of course you boys won't be staying here in the house," he rumbled. "Grant evidently didn't tell you. I wouldn't dare chance bunking you here. Follow along and I'll show you."

He led them down the stairs again, through the dreary hallway into a big kitchen. A woman who was as gaunt and thin as John was fat was taking a roast out of the oven. Her hair was pulled back so tightly that it seemed to be dragging the skin tighter over cheek bones that shone in white peaks. She sniffed at the roast loudly as the men went through the kitchen but gave no glance. As far as she was concerned they did not exist.

John led them through the kitchen into a shed. In the shed he went into a coal bin. He did things to the boards at one side and Barry saw a flight of stairs going down into the darkness.

"Take the boys along," John said to Grant. "You can show them how to get out the other way."

Barry followed Grant down the steps and along a long passage. "The power plant had some underground lines that ran through here years ago. John tapped down and hit them."

They climbed more stairs and came up into a ramshackle building. Through cracks in the sagging roof Barry saw the glint of smoky sky. In one corner were three heaps of straw and some blankets.

"Pretty primitive," Grant said, "but safer than anywhere else we could find." He stared at the piles of straw. "Some of the best of the boys have slept here." He closed his mouth with a snap and his one eye shone. Then he went on: "Most of them are dead. Lots of pressure was brought to bear on some of them. But they never told about this hide-out. So it is still our sanctuary."

They talked for an hour, then John came through the passageway. He was carrying a big basket with a cloth over it and a huge coffee pot. He set them down before the three men and said almost casually, "Couple of tough looking babies just strolled by. They looked kinda of interested in the houses."

Grant said sharply, "Do you think—"

JOHN INTERRUPTED HIM heavily: "Think, hell! You don't waste your time thinking about things like that. You just remember them when you make a move. Fill up, boys. The roast is good. I'll see you when you want me."

When he had gone Grant said harshly: "There goes one of the best guys that ever went afield. Don't let those boiled eyes fool you. He sees a lot more than most people do. He's got a brain as keen as a razor blade. He's getting heavy on his feet now but he can still make very potent magic with a gun. He's a great guy to have with you when the going gets tough."

He munched on a thick sandwich of roast beef and added, "He's only got a few months to live, the doctors tell him. Heart. It's tough. But that's the way it goes."

Joe said, "There's nothing wrong with his ears. He swung around on me with a gun when I wasn't making any more noise than a butterfly's wings touching a flower."

"How about the cook, Sarah?" Barry asked.

"Another one of the old school," Grant answered. "She's been looking after John for a long time. They make a grand team. Sarah has been blind for years. But she sure can get around."

They were in silence for a while, then Barry said, "I suppose we can leave by the other road once it gets dark. I imagine you use this other way only at night."

Grant nodded. "If we used it in the daylight we'd give away our secret. We can pull out when night comes and circulate. How were you planning it?"

"We'll do as we did when we left New York. Slip out, go our own way. You tail me, Joe, and see if anyone spots me. You know your own game, Grant. Better play it your way. We'll meet back here about four in the morning. That's allowing a margin of safety with the darkness. We can sleep here tomorrow. We'll probably need what rest we can get before tomorrow night."

"Yes," Grant added dryly, "we will need our health and strength then. There's a couple of our boys working at the other end of town—if they're still alive. I'll try to contact them and find out if they've picked up anything."

"Let me do the scouting," Barry warned Joe. "You keep strictly out of sight. All you have to do is to watch me. Don't let anyone see you. Okay?"

"Very okay," Joe said emphatically. "I'll play twin to your own shadow."

TWO HOURS LATER Barry slipped like a wraith across the weed-grown vacant lot to another frowsy street. He followed it till he reached a street where the lighted windows of barrooms made glaring attempts to brighten the street.

But behind the lights was something that made them look dim and bleared. The tawdry gaiety was forced and false. It was as though men forced laughter and music to cover the fact that death danced in the streets.

For two hours Barry circulated. Everywhere was the same resentful mutter. But all the men he saw were the workmen, the vast army of men who loved their homes and feared for their city. There was no gangster in evidence. Which was all the more disquieting. If Brisson was keeping them under cover it meant that he was doing it for a purpose. It meant when he unleashed them they would strike swiftly according to a concerted plan.

He was just coming out of a bar when he saw Grant. The one-eyed man was walking down the street, surrounded by a half dozen others. Two of them walked on either side of Grant, hands in their pockets.

Barry fell in a little distance behind them. He did not worry about Joe. He would be at hand when the moment came to strike. And they must strike now. The men who had Grant would torture him to try to make him tell where his two companions were hidden. Barry thought of Brisson and felt cold and tense.

The six men halted beside a big sedan. Barry skirted the building and came opposite the car, standing in a gap between two buildings.

One of the men threw the sedan door open. The other smashed Grant in the jaw, knocking him into the car. The knife Barry flung made a silvery streak in the dim light of the street.

The man yelled hoarsely and threw both arms over his head, falling as he whirled. The man beside him jerked erect, his hand going under his arm. That was the last move he made. The knife handle under his chin jutted out like a slender beard as he threw back his head and staggered. Joe had gone into action. Grant dropped to the sidewalk and started rolling across the pavement. One of the men whipped out a gun and spun toward him.

Firing with cold precision, Barry blasted him. A few yards away Joe's gun belched flame and another of the thugs pitched to the street.

The two others scrambled into the car, trying to pull the door closed behind them. The first one fell out to the street as Barry's slug found him. The other tried to start the car rolling; the door, for which he dared not reach, was swinging wildly. He took a slug in the neck and pitched sideways. The car, now in gear, leaped the pavement and smashed against the side of the building.

Grant leaped to his feet. "I'd hate like hell to have you shooting at me," he said harshly. "You sure do sling lead when you start."

Barry said: "Okay, let's get out of this! We'll have the town around our ears in a minute. These steel town men are just at the lynching stage. They'd probably string us up and ask questions afterwards."

15

TRAIL OF RED

WHILE HE SPOKE Joe ran over to the men and yanked out the two knives. He wiped them hurriedly on the clothes of the dead men, then handed one to Barry. "Always look after your knife," he said dryly. "As a weapon it can't be beaten. It carries an element of surprise that no gun does."

As they ran, Grant gasped: "Both of our operatives are missing. The boys nabbed me when I came here to follow a lead I picked up. The cops in town are paralyzed. Outside of John we three are the sole operatives left alive. Naturally they are tearing the town apart to find us."

"That was crude work they did with you," Barry snapped. "I expected more of Brisson's men."

"They were trying to draw you out," Grant chuckled. "That's why they did the parade with me. They didn't think you'd hit as swiftly and terrifically as you did. That was their hard luck. If Brisson had been with them, I imagine it would have been different. He would have used more finesse."

"I wonder where Brisson is," Barry said. "If I have that fat devil appraised he'll be out on the warpath somewhere."

"Forget it," Joe said harshly. "He didn't catch up with us.

Which is our greatest concern for the moment. Let's go and get some of that sleep. I'm just about dead on my feet."

Which Barry knew was an extravagant overstatement. Joe was made of rawhide and whalebone. He could travel at the rate he had been going for days on end without faltering. But he knew, also, that no one was more careful to conserve energy when there was an opportunity.

As noiselessly and carefully as they had slipped out, they went back to their sanctuary. Sitting on his pile of straw, Barry suddenly remembered something that John Webster had said. "Sometimes I feel that there's a gun muzzle at the back of my neck."

Barry had the hunter's respect for hunches. He knew that if John had that hunch there must be reason for it. He had not spoken idly. He had felt the threat of impending danger.

With the thought Barry leaped to his feet. "Come on," he said to the other two. "Let's take a look at the house."

"John wouldn't like it," Grant objected. "Once we're down here he likes us to stay put. He'll get sore."

"You'd be sorer," Barry snapped, "if you knew that Brisson had caught up with John while we were away. If he spotted the other operatives, why wouldn't he spot John?"

"That's right!" Grant exclaimed.

Before Barry climbed the stairway into the coal bin he halted and listened. He could feel the hair on his neck prickling.

"Do you hear it, Joe?"

Joe's whisper hissed in the darkness: "Yes. Someone is trying to drag himself across the floor. He's moaning as he tries."

Grant snapped, "I'll go ahead. I know how to work that secret door."

But Barry took the lead again as they went through the shed. Moisture oozed from his palm and made the gun butt sticky as if in delirium. He pushed the door open softly and stood poised, ready to kill without mercy or hesitation. **THE FIRST THING** he saw was Sarah, the cook. She was lying on her back in front of the stove, her dead eyes staring at the ceiling, one red hand clutched at the front of her cotton dress. Just across the room a man was lying, beside him a bloody cleaver.

Then he saw John Webster. The big man was dragging himself across the floor. And as he went he left a broad, dark trail behind him. Barry saw the bare feet and felt sick. John's big hands scraped along the boards as he dragged himself toward the dead Sarah.

For a second Barry listened. At his elbow Joe said in a voice that was as thin as wind in a reed: "There's no one else in the house. Whoever did this has gone."

John sagged a little as he turned his wide face toward them. It twisted in a caricature of a smile.

"They caught up to me," he said brokenly. "They knew there was a hide-out somewhere. They asked a lot of questions about it."

He sobbed: "The doctor told me that the old ticker was about done. I thought once or twice that it was going to stop. But it always started pumping again and they brought me back to ask me some more questions."

He seemed to be listening to something away off. "Listen, boys," he said harshly, "do me one favor. There was a guy here tonight I want you to look for. He was a skinny guy with a big Adam's apple and one eye that was cocked out of line. He killed Sarah. Sarah came in and heaved the cleaver before they saw her. She made a bull's-eye on the guy you see over there. The cock-eyed son bumped her. Get him for me, boys."

He sobbed deep in his throat. "Good old Sarah," he said. "She was one swell gal. You owe her that much, boys."

Barry said softly, "We'll do that for you, John. You can depend on that."

"I don't mind what they did to me. In the game, you have to expect to run into things like that. I'm not kicking."

"Was Brisson here?" Barry asked.

John laughed brokenly. "Yes, the pudgy pink and white devil was here. He asked the questions."

He fought for his breath that whistled in his throat. "Crack the thing wide open boys! I'll be looking through the pearly gates rooting for you."

He turned his head and said with great effort, "If you see that doctor again, Grant, tell him he's a dirty lying skunk. He don't know a thing about hearts. If mine had been bad I'd have died long ago. Tell him that for me. Tell him—" He gasped, drew a long deep breath and let it out slowly, brokenly. He shuddered convulsively, then was very still.

Barry was the first to recover himself. With him it was always a matter of his training asserting itself regardless of how profoundly he was moved emotionally. "Let's go," he snapped. "Brisson may come back. There's too much at stake now for us to tangle with him at this stage of the game. Afterward, fellows. After we have cracked this thing, we will have our little inning."

Grant started to pick up a cloth to lay over John's face.

Barry stopped him with an out-thrust hand. "Don't touch anything, Grant. If Brisson comes back don't let him find any sign that we've been here."

He stared at the face of the big man, tortured and twisted in death. "Besides, there's nothing we can do for him now. We have the living to think of."

Grant said in an awed voice. "What kind of a man are you?"

Joe's voice was cold. "Stick with us, Grant, and you'll see what he's made of."

FOR HOURS THE three men sat silently on their piles of straw.

Grant said: "Brisson can kill guys like that. But he can't beat them. And one day we'll catch up to that fat little fiend."

Barry did not answer and Grant went on whispering into the silence. "He was a funny guy, was John. He liked fine things. His big delight was when he got to New York and was listening to the opera and symphonies."

Still Barry did not answer.

Joe growled: "Let's hit the hay. It's getting light. We'll need to be fresh when it gets dark again."

When he awoke, Joe was pouring coffee from the big pot. "I slipped into the kitchen," he said. "Everything is just as we saw it this morning. No one has come in since. I took a chance and boiled some coffee. We'll need it."

They ate in silence and waited for the dark that would be their zero hour.

Suddenly Barry froze alertly. "Listen," he whispered.

He heard far off—so far that Grant could not get it— the dull, throbbing tempo of thousands of marching feet.

"The Paladins are on the go," Joe said softly. "They are marching to the square to hear Carthage."

16

MASS HYSTERIA

UNDER THE WAVERING light of gasoline flares the crowd that massed in the big field on the outskirts of Baxter City swayed and heaved like a restless sea.

Halting in the darkness, Barry stood with Joe and Grant Page, the Federal man, listening.

Joe said: "The bigger it is, the tougher it's going to be for the Unknown and his organization to handle it if a monkey wrench is tossed into the machinery at the right time. We're the fellows elected to do the tossing."

The murmur of the crowd swelled to a thunder of applause as three men mounted the platform.

The leader was in the khaki shirt and trousers of a workman. He walked to the microphones and threw his arms wide in a gesture for silence; and the murmur of the crowd died. His voice roared harshly: "Comrades! Paladins! Tonight I appear, not as your local commander. Tonight I have nothing to say. I come, as all of you have come to listen to the words of our great leader! Comrades! Supreme Commander Carthage!"

It seemed to Barry that the tumultuous roar must bring the stars raining down upon the field. The gasoline flares flickered and wavered, sending writhing serpents of shadows over the sea of upturned faces.

Anthony Carthage made no gestures. He walked to the microphones and stood waiting for the applause to subside. He was a big man, wide-shouldered, straight. A great mane of white hair swept back from his bulging forehead. Even at that distance Barry could feel the power and magnetism.

The applause seemed to sweep backward from the platform as Carthage stared down upon the crowd. His deep-set eyes seemed to be following its retreat across the sea of faces till it died in the fringes of the crowd in ragged ripples and dead silence fell under the dark sky that seemed to be quivering to the billowed roar that had lately risen.

Into that silence Carthage's voice rolled, sonorous, gripping the crowd in its spell. "Paladins of America, I come to speak to you face to face. Heroes of America, I come to bid you be strong and steadfast. The night of terror and lawlessness is closing in upon us. Like these flares that shine in the darkness, so let your courage and integrity shine."

He paused, and not a ripple of sound stirred the silence. But the tension was there. The temper of the crowd was strung to the breaking point.

His voice boomed out again: "Paladins, you are men of tomorrow. Yesterday has vanished. We remember those things that happened yesterday. We live for tomorrow though we cannot forget yesterday. The stench of poison gas still lingers in our memories. The babbling agony of comrades dying in the hospitals still is with us."

The growl of the crowd was like the growl of a great beast; a tremendous, hideous beast that stirs as he wakes from slumber under the prod of spears.

The gun in Brisson's hand roared and searing agony exploded in Barry's head.

"But that belongs to yesterday, comrades! The forces of darkness are not your enemies. They are the enemies of America. They strike at you because you stand for all that is precious and holy and honorable. Remember that, Paladins, and give the nation no opportunity to misjudge your actions."

BARRY FELT JOE stiffen at his side. "It's coming," Joe said harshly. "Listen!"

Barry bent his head. Through the murmur of the crowd, through the far silence of the night, he heard the rushing murmur of powerful cars approaching.

Grant stared at Barry and Joe, his face drawn. He could not hear what they heard.

Barry's voice sounded strange to his own ears. "It's zero hour."

The file of black cars swept through the night without lights, poured down upon the fringes of the crowd in a torrent of destruction. Part of the crowd swung to stare as Carthage's voice paused. For a brief second silence swallowed everything but the powerful t throb of the oncoming motors. Then the silence was blasted wide in a nightmare of horror and confusion.

Grenades made black arcs against the flare of the gasoline torches and burst in orange cones of light. Machine guns chattered. The light of gunfire and bomb explosions outlined the black cars. Then, as swiftly as they had come, the invaders swept away again into the darkness.

The crowd was silent for a second. It was a stunned, sick silence that could only break one way. Through the silence the screams of the wounded cut shudderingly. Then with a roar like surf on a windy shore the voice of the crowd rose.

From the direction of the city came the wail of sirens. Barry felt his lips twitch. The police were coming. In its present temper the crowd would fall upon them and tear them to shreds.

The loudspeakers over the field bellowed. Carthage's voice boomed in deep, commanding tones over the tumult. "Paladins! Listen! Are you men or are you members of a weak rabble? Listen!"

Grant said hoarsely: "Look, he still can handle them!"

On the high platform Anthony Carthage seemed to tower like a colossus. He flung his arms wide and seemed to expand and grow before their eyes. It was a tremendous and dramatic show of personal power and command. His voice was like a trumpet. "Paladins! Listen!"

Little prickles ran up and down the skin of Barry's back. This was something incredible and terrific. This was the supreme demonstration of Carthage's power. The heaving crowd, that seemed on the verge of breaking up and scattering, swayed like a cornfield in a gale. Then it became still. He stood silent under the flickering flares. Carthage's voice seemed to be booming out of the heavens. On the high platform, for the moment, Carthage became a superman, swaying all other men to his will and desire.

"Paladins of America! Men of tomorrow!" His voice died for a second, then intoned its message in driving notes of deep emotion. "The forces of death and lawlessness have struck again. Now the police are coming. Are you going to forget that you are Paladins and become again the scattered and helpless creatures you once were?"

HE PAUSED AS the murmur ran like thunder through the crowd. Then his voice boomed on: "Or are you going to trust me? Are you going to trust me to lead you into a tomorrow where this can never happen again?"

Again he paused as though to let that sink in. "Paladins! I give you my sacred word to lead you into that tomorrow."

The roar that answered him drowned all other sounds. It was as though the three men who listened in the darkness were suddenly engulfed with the flood of emotion that billowed up from the mob.

As the roar died, Carthage went on. "If you hold yourselves like men now, the nation will know that you have the interests of our country at heart. The nation will turn to you, Paladins. Even as I turn to you and command you to stand fast. Tonight drew the curtain on yesterday. Soon you shall hear of tomorrow. Will you trust me, Paladins? Will you wait for the commands I shall send you through your local commanders?"

The voice of the crowd billowed up again. *"Yes!"*

Again he threw both arms outward over the crowd as though in a benediction. His voice rang again like a trumpet. "Paladins of America, stand firm and wait!"

As the three men went down from the platform the crowd burst into frenzied cheering. Out at the edges of the crowds the ambulances were picking up the dead and wounded. But for the second the crowd seemed to have forgotten even that tragedy. They were swaying before the will of one man as a forest sways to the drive of a strong wind.

Barry wiped the back of his hand across a forehead that was clammily wet. Joe drew a long, deep breath and said, "I begin to see."

"Tomorrow," Barry said harshly, "the whole of America will flame with the news of tonight's atrocity. In every village and town the Paladins will wait. They will wait for the orders that Carthage has promised them."

"A perfect plot," Grant said. "Just another move or two and Carthage will have to call upon his Paladins to rescue the nation from chaos. The people as a whole will demand it. Carthage will become a national hero. He'll be sitting on top of the world."

"October Fourth," Barry said bleakly. "Then will occur the explosion that will rock the nation and bring the Paladins to the front as the only force capable of restoring order."

As the three men stood silent in the darkness the Paladins began to move from the field in orderly platoons which marched like companies of drilled soldiers. All this accounted in part for their reaction to Carthage's booming orders. They were soldiers, lacking only arms to be an efficient and powerful army.

Barry had noticed that, after the bombing and shooting, groups of Paladins had immediately turned to the task of caring for the wounded. They had, in other words, even their ambulance units, trained and ready to act.

He was struggling to grasp the tremendous import of the night's demonstration when Joe gripped his arm. "Look!" he snapped. "Look who is going along there!"

17

BREAKING AND ENTERING

THE MAN WAS walking rapidly away from the crowd. For a second he was outlined sharply in the light from the flares. He was tall, and so thin as to be like a caricature of a man. His Adam's apple was huge in his scrawny neck. He turned his head toward the light and Barry saw that the man had a drooping eye.

"The rat that John told us to get!" Grant exclaimed.

"Well, here's once that I get a chance to wipe a mark off."

Barry's voice was sharp. "Wait! Brisson has headquarters here somewhere. This fellow is one of Brisson's personal aides. The chances are he is going to report to Brisson now."

He felt Grant quiver under the touch of his hand. "We'll tail him," he snapped. "Joe, you and Grant follow me."

The thin man walked rapidly toward the jagged skyline of factories that marked the city. Behind him Barry moved like a stalking lobo, as silent as the shadows that hid him. Behind him came Joe and Grant. If the thin man had known that they were at his heels he would probably have broken and run in panic.

Just short of the huge warehouse the thin man halted and spoke in a rumbling murmur to someone in the darkness. Creeping nearer, Barry saw the glint of light on a gun barrel. The man with the gun said something and the thin man walked on toward the building. An oblong of light bloomed as a door was opened. Barry saw the outlines of two more men by the door, saw the guns in their hands, then the door closed.

Joe came out of the darkness and crept beside him. His whisper, breathed into Barry's ear, was exultant: "Looks like we've found something, amigo."

Barry nodded. "Brisson must be there in the building. Also Carthage. And perhaps the big boss. This may be the end of the trail, Joe."

Grant was beside them a moment later when a door opened somewhere grindingly. The door was huge. The creaking it made was massive and metallic. They could only tell that it was somewhere nearby, but not in the building they faced.

While they were trying to locate it, a pair of headlights bloomed in the dark and a motor roared. As though it were a signal, other motors sprang into life, filling the night with their roar.

With a hand on Joe and Grant, Barry moved farther back into the darkness. Crouched in the shadows they waited. The first truck came out of the darkness of the shed with a grinding of gears. It passed them, an immense, gleaming mammoth of the roads. Barry could make out the letters on it as it swept past. *Acme Machinery Company*.

A second truck ground out of the long shed and followed in the wake of the first into the highway. Barry crouched, tense, as twenty-four of the big trdcks rolled out into the road. He remained silent for a long time, listening to the suck of their big tires on the concrete.

The trucks were heavily laden, perhaps with boxes marked machine parts. But honest manufacturers do not guard their plants with platoons of gunmen. Nor do they ship as secretly and quietly as this convoy had been sent out.

Grant whispered, "Arms for the Paladins. That's my guess."

Barry said nothing. But in his heart he was inclined to agree. And, if this shipment were that, there must have been hundreds more like them trundling over other roads. For if one section of the Paladins was to be armed, all would be.

"ONE THING GETS me," Joe whispered. "Where does the army come in on this? The police may be partly demoralized. But the State police and militia present a formidable army. If Carthage is working this way, he is only heading for a civil war that he must lose in the end."

Barry shook his head slowly. "There's more to it than that. October Fourth figures into this somewhere. Whatever is planned for that day is the move that is supposed to make the whole plan workable. That's the thing we've got to find out. Once we put our hands on that, all the truck loads of ammunition and guns in creation won't help Carthage."

"The secret is there in the building where the thin man vanished," Grant said shrewdly.

"Then we'll have a look," Barry decided. "The outer ring of guards will be easy to pass. But there'll be men on every entrance. We'll have to work this smoothly. One slip and the whole thing will blow up in our faces!"

He rose slowly. "Grant, take the rear. Making a hole

through the line without any fuss is a little specialty of Joe's and mine. We make the hole, then we all go through."

The guards were twenty feet apart. Barry crept so close to one that he could have touched him. The guard seemed to sense that someone was near. He turned slowly.

As he bent forward, Barry moved with a speed that the eye could not follow. The side of his hand chopped down on the fellow's neck and he dropped as though he had been shot.

Joe was under him as he fell to ease his weight down noiselessly. Barry stepped over the man and walked toward the building. There he stopped for a moment in the shadows while he whispered, "You, Grant, stay out here in case Joe and I slip when we get inside. Joe, you and I will find a side door. There'll be guards there. We'll try to take them without fuss. Once inside we go on our own. Right?"

"Right!" Joe whispered, and Grant's reply was a breathed echo.

They found the side door. Crouched in the darkness they could hear the nervous whispering of the two guards. Barry smiled thinly as he listened to what they were saying.

"I don't like this job," one was muttering. "They tell me that these guys ain't human. One minute there's no one there, then, *pow!*—and you're missing your head or something. I don't like it."

"You'll like it a hell of a sight less if the boss hears you beefing that way. The boss doesn't like chin music about those guys."

The first one snarled: "And why? Because those guys took a coupla falls outa him and he's sore as a pup."

Barry inched forward. When he halted, flattened against

the building, he was less than a couple of yards from the guards. On the other side of the doorway, he knew, Joe would be waiting, as tense and ready as a coiled snake.

He tossed one of the pebbles he had picked up against the wall of the neighboring building. The stone made a sharp click against the brick wall and both guards whirled. The nervous one took a step forward as the second pebble clicked.

"HEY," HE WHISPERED hoarsely, "do you think we oughta call the boss?"

"And get our pants kicked for being scared of ghosts? Now, that ain't nothin'. Beetles against the wall."

"Beetles, hell!" the other one snapped. "Whoever heard of beetles this time of year?"

"Well, it's somethin' like that," the second man insisted. "Go tell the boss if you want to. I ain't askin' for any trouble like that."

The first man took a pace forward, gun at his hip, his head thrust forward, Barry struck. The man gave a sobbing grunt and pitched forward.

The second guard leaped. Joe came out of the dark like a panther. One hand snapped across the man's mouth, as the knife in the other came down in a glittering streak. Joe eased his man to the ground and whispered, "Well, I guess we get in. Let's go."

Barry whispered, "Give me a minute's start, then come in and cover my trail."

The steps from the doorway led down into a maze of basement corridors. Working toward the front of the building, Barry threaded his way between cement walls that oozed chill dampness. If Brisson and Carthage were in the building, he figured, they would be somewhere above. And with them was the secret of October Fourth and the trucks that had rolled out of the big shed.

He mounted the flight of cement steps as softly as a prowling cat. He turned the knob of the door at the top softly, and eased the door open an inch at a time. He stepped through into a big, open space, and froze, listening.

To his left was a long sliver of dim light under a door. Behind that door Barry knew he would find Brisson. He heard Joe come up the stairs behind him, but did not turn his head. His muscles ran like oil under his skin as he crossed to the door under which shone the light.

Just as he had opened the door behind him, so he now eased the door toward him slowly and soundlessly. When it stood open he waited tensely. Far away sounded the trembling echoes of a voice.

18

WILL O' THE WISP

GAZING THROUGH THE door, he felt himself stiffen. He was looking into the interior of a huge warehouse, which was dimly lighted by lamps that hung high overhead. The big warehouse was filled from end to end with squat armored cars and cases of what he knew would be guns and ammunition.

The cases of ammunition were piled like mountains toward the maze of rafters and beams that made a network overhead. This was, without a doubt, the stuff with which Carthage's Baxter City Paladins were to be armed when the real zero hour was called.

At the other end of the room two men were standing. As Barry watched them they paced down an aisle cleared through the middle of the warehouse. And as they went their eyes searched the shadows around them.

Barry hid behind one of the mountains of cases and waited. The two men reached the door through which he had just come, turned and walked back again.

All the time Barry's eyes were probing every corner of the building. The thin man had come in here. He had undoubtedly come to report to Brisson. Therefore Brisson must still be in the building. Then Barry spotted it, down at the other end—a room set on a sort of platform. All that marked it was a thread of light under a door. Then he made out the stairway leading up from the other end of the building.

To get up that stairway would be next to impossible. There were the two men who were evidently on guard. Outside, the darkness swarmed with guards. Undoubtedly there were others up there in the room with Brisson. Then he noticed the hanging cable of the crane that was used to pile up the ammunition boxes. The iron hook on the end hung about on a level with his head.

Waiting until the two men were pacing away from him, Barry reached for the cable. He caught it in fingers that were as strong as steel claws. Hand over hand he went up the cable. He was squatting on an iron girder far overhead when the two men started back.

Waiting again until the two men were walking away from him, Barry ran lightly along the girder toward the platform and the door with its sliver of light. He halted on the girder, flattened against the wall of the room, watching the two guards who silently paced the tiny platform at the head of the stairs. Brisson was taking all precautions.

With his eyes glued to a tiny crack in the wall, Barry saw them. Brisson was standing beside a long table with the thin man directly behind him. Just beyond Brisson, Carthage was standing. His mane of white hair shone like burnished silver under the hanging light bulb. But just now he was looking at the figure whom he recognized as boss. His acknowledgment was in every line of his face; in the way he stood and listened.

The figure he watched was cloaked in black. A black robe

covered him, muffling his figure. It was impossible to tell whether the man was fat or thin. On his head was a black hood that covered his face and muffled his voice.

He talked in an indistinguishable monotone. Even here among his trusted lieutenants he took no chances of exposure. His voice came clearly to Barry. "You have your orders, Carthage. Are your Paladins ready?"

"After tonight," Carthage said harshly, "they'll do anything I tell them. After tonight it won't be a question of prodding them in. It will be a case of trying to hold them back till the appointed time."

WITHOUT MOVING, THE black-robed figure asked: "And you, Brisson? Are all our arrangements complete? Are your men prepared and ready to carry through their end of the game?"

Brisson's blue eyes shone like sapphires in the light. His red lips parted in a confident grin. "Everything is set. From here to California my men are ready. Every detail of time has been figured out. They'll strike simultaneously on the hour. You can trust me, Chief."

There was an ominous edge to the muffled voice. "I trusted you to wipe Gerald Sanderson, alias Barry Chase, out of the picture. And what happened?"

Brisson shivered and his fat face went dead and hard. The blue eyes seemed to lose their luster and the lips thinned into a pencil line of red.

"Three times you had your chance, Brisson. And three times you let him make a fool of you. I'd hate to have that happen again."

Brisson shivered imperceptibly. "He isn't human," he said thickly. "He and that damned Indian are a couple of ghosts. I tell you I had everything fixed and they slipped through my fingers like water."

The hooded head shook slowly. "Excuses won't do, Brisson. I know that the two of them are smart. I thought you were similarly endowed. It seems that I was mistaken."

Brisson seemed to shrink under the stare from the hooded figure. Then the muffled voice went on: "Your arrangements are all made. But I tell you both, our plans are as insecure as cob webs in a March gale as long as Barry Chase and the Indian are alive. You've got to find them, Brisson."

He was silent for a second, his hooded head bowed. Then he raised it slowly. "We may be able to keep our secret from him until the zero hour. If we don't find him that's our only chance."

"You have your prisoner," Brisson said harshly. "We could use the girl to pull him into the open."

"You've been seeing too many movies, Brisson," the hooded man said icily. "Chase is too smart to put himself into our hands to save the girl. He proved that in Irontown. At that time we had no idea of his brains and guile. We thought we had him. And he was playing with us. He made fools of us all. But that should have warned you, Brisson."

From beneath the hood his laughter came snarlingly. "Why, you fat muddler, he could have killed you on two occasions. The first time he made a mistake by allowing you to go. But now I wonder if it was such a mistake. He's been on our heels most of the time, following you to me." The black mask leaned far over the table as the muffled voice boomed, "Do you know where he is at this instant?"

BARRY EASED THE gun from under his arm and waited

tensely. The hooded man was smart as Satan, and he was as wary as a fox.

As though in answer to the question a door below flung open with a thunderous bang. A man raced through, stopped and yelled: "They're in the building! They killed the two guys on the side door and got in!"

Barry's heart leaped: He might be caught. But there was one thing he could do. He lifted the snout of the gun and put it against the crack. He could kill the man in the hood.

But with the first yell of alarm the hooded man was in motion. With a convulsive heave he threw himself sideways out of the chair just as Barry's gun roared.

Barry saw the black cloak jerk as the slug flicked high up on the right shoulder. Cursing, the man ran from the room.

Barry was racing back along the iron beam toward the center girder when he heard Brisson yell shrilly, a catch of hysteria in his voice. "Lights! Throw those switches, you damned fools! We'll get him this time. He can't get near the lines to cut them!"

The guns of two men below Barry roared. They had looked up and spotted the blur of motion he made in the darkness.

He turned once as leaden slugs beat a thunderous tatoo on the beam beneath his feet. One of the men on the platform had spotted him. His own gun roared and the man on the platform tipped over the rail and fell headlong to the floor. He heard a gun blast below and the man who was firing at him with a machine gun doubled up. That would be Joe cutting into the game.

Barry picked the second man off the platform with his

second shot and ran farther along the beam just as light came on in a white blaze.

Below him other men were running through the open door. He froze for a second on the girder, then chuckled in cold mirth. The lights were hung below him, reflectors throwing the light down to flood the men below in a white blaze of dazzling brilliance.

He saw Joe running along behind the row of armored cars, making for the crane tackle up which Barry had scrambled to reach the girders. Joe could make it if Barry could create a diversion to cover him.

Barry ran lithely back toward the platform where the two men had been stationed. He paused, dropped to lay flat on the girder, and blasted at the men below him.

They whirled and stared upward, trying to locate the flash of the gun in the cavernous blackness above the lights. But the flood of brilliance they had arranged to trap him should he enter the building now worked against them. Staring up, they could see nothing. The light poured into their eyes, blinding them, hiding anything that was above in gloom.

THE AUTOMATIC KICKED against the heel of his hand as he worked the trigger. Below him a man with a machine gun turned around slowly, to fall forward on his face.

Joe was coming up the cable hand over hand. But all eyes for the moment were trying to find the elusive phantom who once more had thrown confusion among them.

One of them turned and saw Joe. His yell of alarm was high and shrill. It banged from wall to wall in hysterical echoes. Then it was drowned in the crashing roar of gunfire. Barry felt his throat constrict. His heart was a dead lump in his chest. Joe looked tiny, clinging to the swaying cable in the glare of the lights. Just over his head was the rim of shadow that waited to envelop him. But below him the machine gun in the hands of the thug raised its voice in a chant of death.

For a second Barry fired hastily, thrown from his granite calm by the sight of Joe's danger. Then his arm grew as steady as the long years of training steadied his heart and brain. He drew a deep breath and shot with cool precision and another of Brisson's men pitched forward.

Joe paused briefly beside him, crouching low on the girder. "What's the next move?"

"Brisson! Carthage! And the mysterious man in the black robe!" Barry snapped. "They were in a room at the other end of the warehouse."

He ran along a cross-beam and came to the platform leading to the room where the conference had been held. He leaped the railing, landed on tip-toes and without hesitation launched himself at the throat of the man who came up the stairway.

Barry's automatic made a dull, crunching sound as he brought it down savagely on the gangster's forehead. The man dropped without a sound, his gun banging dully on the boards.

For a second Barry stood silent, his head thrust forward listening. From below came a babel of excited sounds. Men yelling shrill excitement. They saw fancied movements above them in the shadows and their guns made thundering, crashing punctuations to their yells.

"Inside!" Barry snapped. "They'll get their heads in a few minutes and rush the stairway in a mass. Right now

I want to look for the mystery man and his henchmen. I imagine they've gone. But maybe we can crack down on them before they get far."

He jerked the door open and flung himself into the conference room. The bulb over the desk made a cone of light where the masked man had leaned a few minutes before.

The room beyond the open door was like the one they had entered, empty. Joe found the narrow door that opened on a stairway going steeply down.

AT THE FOOT of the stairs they halted. Beyond them was the open, crawling with Brisson's hirelings. The gunners would be waiting for the first sign of motion at any of the building's exits. A motor roared and headlights cut swaths in the night as a car shot away from the building.

"There they go," Joe whispered harshly. "They've beaten us by a jump again."

Barry touched Joe on the arm and slipped out of the door. One moment he was a blur, the next he was a dozen yards away, standing bent-kneed, listening to the staccato hammers of the guns flinging lead at the spot he had left a second before.

He ran along the building and crouched in an angle made by a jutting ell, waiting. In half a minute Joe flowed like a heavier segment of darkness to take his position beside him.

Barry whispered, "Grant! Where is he?"

They found Grant a few hundred yards back. He said: "I was beginning to worry. I did a pussyfoot circle of the building to see if I could spot you making a break and do a little helping. I just got here in time to horn in."

Bitterness crept into his voice. "I didn't get back here in

time to throw a slug into Brisson and his pets. I saw them as they reached their car but they were too far away for me to do anything about it."

"It was the gathering of the clan all right," Joe said. "What did you hear up there in the room?"

"Nothing," Barry said. "Except that the fuse is laid and the spark is ready. And they've gone with their knowledge."

"We can guess where they'd go," Grant said softly.

"Carthage's watch tower?" snapped Barry.

Grant grunted. "Yes. Up in the woods beyond Culverton. I've seen it. A tough place to get into. He planned it for just such an emergency as this."

"Let's take a look at it. It's only a hundred and fifty miles. If we drive fast we can get there in time to do something before daylight comes."

Joe remarked thinly, "Did you notice that the cops didn't come to this little picnic? They ignored the racket this time. They must be getting scared."

"After what happened earlier they should be scared," Barry snapped., "Now, where do we get a car?"

Grant said eagerly, "John had one. He kept it in a garage behind the lodging house. We could use that."

They got the car and drove away in the darkness, headed for the famous watch tower of Carthage in the lonely country beyond Culverton. Something hammered on Barry's brain with deadening persistence. Some inner sense was trying to warn him of something; trying to tell him of something that he should know. And it was connected in some way with the hooded figure at the table in the warehouse.

But the thought of the girl made him fight down the presentiment.

19

THE TRAP

A MILE FROM their goal they left the car and went on foot toward the famous tower from which Carthage's voice poured nightly to his listening million of scattered Paladins.

Just outside the huge gate-posts that reared their gray granite columns in the darkness, they halted. There was no light, no sign of life in the building. As they crept closer, Joe's voice hissed in Barry's ear: "Something wrong here. The place looks deserted."

They slipped through the open iron gates. There were no signs of the guards who usually stood on duty day and night. Nothing stirred.

At the end of the hedge Barry froze. The big front door of the house gaped open. At the foot of the steps a man was lying sprawled, face down. Another was at the top, his head and shoulders hanging over the treads.

Barry made no move to touch them. When Grant stepped toward the stone stairs, Barry thrust out a detaining hand. "Wait! There's something wrong with the set-up. If Carthage's guards are dead it's because he sold them out as he sold out the men who were killed at the Baxter City mass meeting tonight. It's another move in their game that's so damnably deep and dark."

"You think it's another trap?" Grant asked sharply.

"Stop and think a minute, Grant. If you had been Brisson or his boss tonight what would you expect us to do?"

"This was the obvious thing."

"Exactly," Barry said bitterly. "They knew we'd come. So a bunch of Brisson's men made a raid on the place and cleaned up. And Carthage is setting up another headquarters. Tomorrow this will be public news. Carthage's station raided. His guards killed. Probably his sending apparatus wrecked. Another rasp on the already sensitive skins of the Paladins.

"By tomorrow Carthage will be broadcasting from a new point, pushing his Paladins a little closer to the explosion that he intends to use for his own ends."

"Aren't you going in?" Grant asked sharply.

"Not by that open door," Barry answered. "It is just a little too inviting. Since we are here we might just as well enter, but rather less obtrusively."

He waited a minute, keen ears straining to catch some sign or sound. Then he whispered. "There are men in that building. I can hear them."

"Plenty of them," Joe whispered. "They expected us to walk in. They're waiting for us."

"But Brisson won't be there," Barry guessed. "I'll bet my life on that. Brisson knew we would come here, and he set a trap for us."

They circled the silent tower. At the back Barry whispered, "I can climb that angle of the wall. Instead of going in at the bottom we'll hit the top and work down."

"Sorry," Grant said bitterly, "but human fly stuff isn't in my line."

Barry said promptly: "We should have a man outside to cover us in any event. Joe and I will go in. I'll go first. Joe, follow as soon as you see me get to the top."

Grant breathed, "Good hunting!"

BARRY TRIED TO make his climbing soundless, but it was difficult. His clothing rasped on the stones. If anyone with the ears of Joe or himself had been listening they would have heard him before he had climbed three yards.

At the top of the tower he rested. When Joe was beside him he breathed in his ear, "I'm going to cross the roof to that window over there. There's a trap door in the roof here, but we'd wake the dead getting it up."

He slid across the slate roof to the window he had pointed out. He got it open with no trouble and slipped noiselessly into the room. In the faint light that came through the window he studied the bedroom, which was plainly furnished, probably the sleeping quarters of one of the guards. There was nothing here to interest him.

With Joe beside him he opened the door softly and slipped out into the hallway. Thick carpets covered the flagged floor; made extreme caution unnecessary.

Yet even as he moved in the silent house, Barry was conscious of the pounding warning in his brain again. He had thought it a trap. Now he believed it was more than that. Behind this mystery lay another move on the part of the wily boss who ordered the doings of Brisson and Carthage. Another move in the game of chess that the boss was playing on the map of America with men's lives for pawns.

Barry leaned against the rail of the balcony that overlooked the great, dim hall below. He could hear someone whispering. The voice came to him clearly and sharply. "I tell you this is screwy! Why did Casden give us orders to crash this joint anyway? We kill a lot of guards and squat here in the dark for a couple of guys that will maybe come. How do we know they will come? It begins to look to me like we're being used for suckers."

As Barry backed away from the railing Joe came to his side, pulled him farther back against the wall, and whispered, "There's something about this that smells. I found the control room. Nothing has been touched. Carthage's office is as neat as if he'd just walked out of it. There's a narrow stairway going up to a tower room. The door at the top is locked. Want to try it?"

Barry nodded and followed Joe up the stairway. Joe took a slim leather case from his pocket, opened it and went to work on the door. In two minutes he pushed the door open and the two stood listening.

Barry could smell death there in the room. Cautiously he slid over the threshold and entered. By the faint light filtering through a high, barred window he saw a huddled figure on the floor.

Leaving Joe at the door, Barry crossed the room and squatted beside the figure. It was cold. From his pocket he took a pencil flashlight and snapped it on. The man had been tortured as John Webster had been tortured. And, just as John Webster had been left to die in lingering agony, so this man had been left. Then Barry caught his breath. One gory hand was outstretched on the flagged floor. The stiffened fingers rested at the end of a series of clumsy letters.

Barry read them. The man had written them with his own blood on the floor of his cell. "Not 4—tomorrow nite—Bris…" The letters trailed off in a thin smear.

Joe came to look over Barry's shoulder. Barry heard his breath hiss through his clenched teeth. "One of our boys," breathed Joe. "Brisson or Carthage brought him here and tortured him. But the boy learned something."

Barry whispered: "Not 4. That means the gang is scared and is going to hurry things. The break comes tomorrow night."

He jerked erect as the thin wail of far sirens came to his ears.

20

DISASTER

IN THE HALL below someone said hoarsely: "The cops! To hell with this! I'm pulling out. They don't mow me down."

Barry said, "I begin to see. Carthage's place raided. He calls the cops. He'll be with them, I'll bet. And he'll be boiling with righteous wrath. Tomorrow night is the break. He'll broadcast tonight. He'll sound the alarm and have his Paladins standing by."

The sirens came screaming up the road as the thugs below rushed out into the darkness. Racing to a window at the front, Barry watched the long line of headlights come hurtling through the darkness.

He whirled and snapped at Joe, "You found Carthage's office. Lead me to it."

The two crossed the quiet magnificence of the office as the sirens wailed to a halt outside. Flinging the window wide, Barry glanced out. He motioned to Joe, who stepped through and stood on the wide ledge at one side of the window, clinging with crooked fingers to a rough piece of granite.

Barry halted long enough to hear Carthage's resonant voice: "I was in the car as the desperados drove up. My chauffeur had the presence of mind to drive away without turning on the headlights. I went directly to you."

A voice said, "Looks like they killed your guards. Any idea who they were?"

"They were undoubtedly part of the same gang that seems bent on destroying our organization. This, Captain, is the end. From this time on my Paladins will really defend themselves."

The Captain's voice was nervous. "This is bad, Mr. Carthage. What do you want me to do? Shall I put a guard on your place?"

"No," Carthage said oratorically. "I only wanted you to see for yourself what is happening. I wish you would report this. But I am not afraid. I have brought more of my Paladins. They will guard me. If you will see that the dead guards are taken back to Culverton I will arrange for the funerals."

Barry stepped through the window and stood across from Joe on the ledge. He pushed the window closed with his toe and waited. Light bloomed inside the wide window.

Carthage crossed the room and dropped heavily into the big chair before the desk. His back was to the window.

A thin man came into the room and faced Carthage. His voice came to Barry. "I have the men on the control room. In two minutes you go on the air. We timed it perfectly. Before the raid we made the announcement that you would speak at two A.M. Are you ready?"

Carthage's resonant voice had the faintest quaver of fear in it. "I don't like hurrying things this way."

"It isn't what you like," the thin man said harshly. "It's what the boss orders. Chase and the Indian have him worried. He knows that we've got to put this over within the next twenty-four hours or the whole plan may go bust."

A man thrust his head in the door behind the thin man and gasped, "Someone busted in the tower room. The guy is dead. But the door is open."

As Barry cursed himself for forgetting to close the door the thin man snarled: "All right, it's open. Call in a dozen men and have them go over the house from top to bottom. Tell them to shoot without warning if they spot anything. You," he snapped at Carthage, who had stood up with a jerk, "sit down and start broadcasting."

THE THIN MAN walked to the desk, pushed a microphone in front of Carthage and said harshly, "Start broadcasting. Don't get jittery." He reached over and threw a switch on the side of the desk.

Barry nodded at Joe, flung the window wide and leaped into the room with a single fluid snap. The thin man's mouth sagged open, then his hand snapped under his lapel. It stayed there as the thrown knife hissed over Barry's shoulder and caught him in the throat.

Joe went past Barry in a tigerish leap and closed the door. He turned the key in the lock and swung around, gun in his hand, his bronze face hard and bitter in the light.

With a swift motion, Barry reached over and cut the switch as he held the muzzle of his gun against Carthage's neck. His voice crackled in the empty room. "Carthage, you're going on the air and tell your Paladins to be patient and wait for further orders. And you're going to stall them off. There'll be no orders to arm tomorrow night. Maybe your local commanders have those orders. But you're going to tell every one of them listening now that the word is 'patience.' You're going to tell them that they must take no orders until they hear from you again. Now, talk! And if you slip, just as sure as you sit in that chair, you get a bullet through the back of your head. I mean that, Carthage."

Carthage reached a trembling hand for the microphone as Barry threw the switch. Carthage's voice had an uncertain quaver in it as he started to talk.

But listening, Barry felt admiration for this shrewd demagog. His voice took on its rolling resonance. He was talking himself out of the shadow of death and he knew it. Sweat rolled down his cheeks as he told his Paladins to wait for another tomorrow, to stand firm and wait for the word of their supreme commander.

Listening, Joe's face cracked in a sardonic grin. Barry felt the cold lump in his chest dissolving. The coup, he reasoned, might still be pulled tomorrow night. But Carthage's speech would certainly throw the whole vast plot into temporary confusion and give them a few precious hours in which to find Brisson and spike his guns.

Carthage's daily broadcasts usually lasted fifteen minutes. Barry watched the clock on the wall tick off the minutes. He could hear his own pulses hammering in his ears.

Before the broadcast was finished men were hammering on the door. Carthage's voice rolled on sonorously. At the end of the period he leaned back in his chair, his face ashen, hands trembling.

Barry leaned forward and snapped off the switch again. "You may try to talk your way out of that, Carthage. But I don't think you will. You've slipped. You've crossed Brisson and the big boss. I wouldn't like to be in your shoes now."

"Now," Barry went on relentlessly, "you are going out with us. Out the window, Carthage, if it breaks your smooth neck. Out there in the darkness we'll have a little talk. It will be somewhere quiet, Carthage, where no one can hear you scream. For you may scream before you decide to talk and tell us who your boss is,"

Barry jerked around as the door across the room opened. Carthage threw himself forward on the floor as Joe's gun roared. The man who had opened the door fell into the room on his face. Behind him there were other men.

Behind them Brisson's shrill voice screamed, "Don't let them get away!"

Barry threw three shots through the door and the men fell back. He jerked his head toward the window and Joe crossed the room and swung over the sill. Barry turned and shot at Carthage, just as the big man rolled behind a huge filing cabinet.

Then Barry followed Joe. He caught the sill with his fingertips and lowered himself. Just as he started down he saw Brisson, demoniacal with rage, leap into the room. The gun in Brisson's hand roared and searing agony exploded in Barry's head. For one awful instant he felt himself falling, then darkness engulfed him as the world dissolved in the roaring tumult around his ears.

21

THE HOODED MAN

BARRY GROPED TO the surface of consciousness. Someone had a hand over his mouth. Someone was holding his arms as he struggled. Then he heard Grant's voice saying softly, "Easy, boy! Easy, boy! Easy does it."

He sat up slowly and held his throbbing head in his hands as Grant released him. A thousand hammers of pain were banging on his head. White flames danced in front of his eyes.

Grant's voice went on: "I thought for a second that they had potted you. But it's okay. A slug parted your hair. You'll be all right in a jiffy. Here, take a drink of this."

Grant held the bottle to his lips. Red hot liquid trickled down his throat and made him gag. But the pale flames died before his eyes and the hammers that banged on his skull had pads on them now and didn't hurt with such shocking agony.

"How long was I out?" he whispered as he took his hands down from his head and tried to see Grant in the impenetrable darkness.

"Just a few minutes," Grant whispered. "Luckily Joe and I were under you when you fell and saved you from a broken neck."

Gradually, as consciousness became clearer and sharper, Barry realized that he was in a darkened room. Rough stone at his back and rough concrete beneath him told him that it was a basement. He wondered where he was and how long since he had left the room in which Carthage had made his broadcast.

Grant's whisper told him: "You've been out for about fifteen minutes. When you dropped from the window the gang started to swarm out to look for us. There was a basement window. We slipped in and left the Paladins scouring the countryside. Evidently some of Brisson's gangsters hung around to see what would happen. When the blow-off came they beat it with the Paladins at their heels. That was our break. Right now they are looking everywhere but where we are, inside the watch tower."

As the pain in his head subsided and became at last only a burning gash where the slug had furrowed, Barry began to think as the hunter once more. Right now the bulk of the Paladins would be out combing the countryside.

Grant said: "The gangsters had cars parked out of sight. They reached them and made their getaway. The Paladins did not catch up with them and we'll get the credit of a snappy retreat. It gives us a chance. Right now Joe is out doing a prowl."

Waiting for Joe to return, Barry sat silently in the darkness, gathering strength and clarity of thought. As he rested, his mind went back over the whole of this incredible adventure into which he had been pitchforked on his arrival in New York. Never, in his wildest dreams of adventure, had he imagined anything on this scale.

He thought of Bill Cleghorn and the Gray Man. They

had prepared him well for this game that was so much bigger than anything they could have foreseen. At the same time he was conscious of a deep and abiding satisfaction. The enemy of his own that he must run to earth if he were ever to be a free man again, was also the arch enemy of his country.

So softly did Joe move that Grant was not conscious of his presence until he whispered thinly in the darkness. Barry felt Grant's start of surprise, and smiled as the one-eyed man said: "You damned copper-colored ghost. I hope you never start pussy-footing on my trail."

Joe chuckled. "I went up through the hall. It's dimly lighted. I passed two Paladins so closely that I could have touched them and they didn't know I was within a mile of them."

"The big boss is here?" Barry's whispered question was edged and bleak.

"I don't know, kid," Joe said huskily. "But I think he is. I think he's in the office with Carthage and Brisson." He shivered and went on. "I smell trouble in this house, Barry. I smell something like death. And there's someone in the tower room. The door is guarded by one of the Paladins. It may be Moreland or it may be the girl, or both."

Barry stood up in the darkness and stretched his arms.

"We have a couple of hours of darkness left. The last two hours in which to work, fellows. If we slip tonight the smash will come tomorrow and we will have failed. We've got to move swiftly."

The lights came on in a blaze in the basement room as Brisson's voice bubbled mirthfully: "No, my dear young friend, you have not two hours left. You are through." His fat, cherubic face smiled at them.

BARRY STOOD IN the center of the room where the lights had caught him. No trace of his inner sickness showed on his face. His gray eyes were icily bleak as he met Brisson's cherubic smile.

Brisson stood in the door, a big automatic in his hand. On one side of him a man in a Paladin uniform was standing, a sub-machine gun in his hands.

Brisson's voice dripped pleasure. "You know you begin to bore me. I had expected you to vanish in a puff of smoke this time. Returning to the basement while we searched for you outside was clever. Not so clever was your copper-colored helper's prowling. He did it very well, but not well enough to escape me when he passed through the hall. I could have killed him then. But it gave me more pleasure to allow him to lead me to your hiding place."

He looked at the guns on the floor and his smile broadened. "This time I take no chances. Reach for the guns if you wish. Before you touch them you will be dead. In the hall behind me are three more men with machine guns."

He shook with the mirth that consumed him. "There are no lights to be snapped off this time, my playful boy. There is nothing for you now but death."

He stepped to one side as three men pushed past him into the room. They ran quick hands over the three captives, stripping them of guns and knives.

Grant's good eye was imploring Barry. It was death anyway. Why not death in battle? Better, his single eye said eloquently, to go down fighting than die like sheep.

But there was something in Barry's glance that said,

"Wait!" Something that said, "There's more to this than any mere capture." So Grant waited.

Brisson sighed gently as the three men he hated backed to the wall, stripped of all the weapons they could use so well, "Now, my friends, we shall spend a pleasant few minutes above. You will walk out slowly, following the men who will lead the way. I shall walk behind you with the others. It will give me the keenest pleasure to shoot you in the back should you try to make a break. March!"

Carthage was behind his big desk, his ever-present guard at his back. His lips twisted in a smile.

"Splendid!" he boomed.

No sign of the man of mystery.

Brisson stared at Barry with all the false mirth flowing out of his face. He walked to the wall and turned a knob.

A panel slid back in the ceiling and Barry felt a sick chill creep through him. A man was on his knees, resting his weight on the hands that were fastened in front of him with heavy manacles. Frederick Moreland.

Moreland straightened with an effort. Then Barry saw that he was naked to the waist, his breast criss-crossed with horrible red welts. His mouth sagged open as he stared with wide eyes. He threw himself forward toward the gap that the panel left and raised his voice in a shout.

Brisson turned the knob and the panel slid back. "If we could do that to Moreland, who constituted only a slight disturbance in our lives, think what we shall do to you," he said brightly.

He licked his red lips. "I look forward to a session with you in the room above, my dear young friend. I look forward to it with more eagerness than I can convey to you."

JOE STOOD STOLIDLY. In his pose was something that Grant could not understand. He let his chin rest on his chest and gazed somberly at the floors waiting for what Grant did not know. It was as though he were waiting for a sign from Barry. Brisson glanced at him and seemed to find the sight amusing.

He chuckled merrily and chirped, "Dear me, our stolid Indian seems not to be perturbed. We shall see if we cannot change that. Up above we shall tackle you and break that mask. I'm sure we shall."

Grant said, "Why don't you shut up, or else get a man to talk for you, Brisson? Your sweet girlish voice gets on my nerves. Shut up or do something."

Something demoniac shone in Brisson's eyes. The hand holding the gun shot forward and his finger tightened on the trigger. Then Brisson straightened with a jerk. "You almost fooled me that time, Page. You almost fooled me into giving you a merciful bullet. I shan't let you do it again. There is nothing so nice for you as sudden death."

He jerked around as the door at the other end of the room opened and a black-garbed figure came into the room. He stood beside Carthage at the desk and stared at the three men.

His muffled voice said, "I am glad to see you all here gentlemen." The loose fold of the hood that hung before his face swayed as he turned toward Brisson. "I congratulate you on the efficiency of your work, Brisson. For a little while I doubted that you had their plans so well anticipated."

There was real respect mingled with the gloating triumph in Brisson's voice. "They fooled me before because the tactics they used were new. When the novelty had worn off, their machinations became very apparent. Then I had only to anticipate."

"Your one great weakness, Brisson," the cloaked man said in his muffled voice, "is vanity. You like to gloat, don't you? Well, under the circumstances I suppose you have the right."

His gloved hands trembled a little as he rested them on the desk beside Carthage. "It's been a long trail, Sanderson. I suppose you've often wondered why I followed you for so long. You don't know what it is to hate, Sanderson." His voice got thicker and furrier. "You don't know what it is to hate a man so much that you want to tear out every last root of his family. You don't know what it is to hate a man so much that you can never rest nor sleep soundly till you know that he and his line have been completely exterminated. You don't know what hate like that is, do you, Sanderson?"

"Not hate," Barry said calmly. "Fear! You were afraid of my father. If it wasn't fear you would tear off your mask now."

The muffled voice under the hood was thick with a passion that raked along Barry's nerves. "Perhaps it was fear. If so it was as potent as is hate. It served its purpose. It kept me on your track for years. It has led me to you at last. And this time you won't get away."

Barry smiled thinly. "Don't be so sure! I'm far from dead this moment. Aren't you afraid right now that I'll pull a gun out of nowhere? I might do that, you know. If you weren't afraid you would let me see your face. You won't show it now because you think there is a chance that I'll get away and hunt you down. You're afraid."

For a second the gloved hand clutched the folds of the black hood that hung in front of his face. Barry leaned forward. Then the gloved hand dropped.

The voice behind the mask was calm and even again. "You almost succeeded that time, Sanderson. But it wasn't fear that stopped me. It was merely sane caution. But you shall see my face. I promise you that. You shall see my face before you die."

He turned his head and spoke to Brisson. "Take them above, put cuffs on them, and lock them in the tower room. Take no chances. When they are shackled meet me in this office."

He seemed to be considering the position. As Brisson and the gunmen backed away, their guns trained on Barry, the hooded man seemed to change his mind. "I shall go up with you," he said suddenly. "I want to see them shackled."

22

THE UPPER ROOM

THEY WENT UP the narrow stairway, two men walking behind each of them, gun muzzles prodding into their backs. In the tower room Barry let his breath out in a soft hiss. The black stains where the secret service man had bled were still on the stone floor. But Moreland was gone.

As though reading his thoughts, the hooded man said, "Your friend Moreland has been removed. Since each of you are more important to us than Moreland, we moved him to other quarters."

His chuckle was thick and hoarse. "We have Miss Darrow, too. I shall not subject her to the horror of looking at you when we have finished persuading you to talk."

Brisson smiled, sighed softly, and directed two of his men to manacle the prisoners.

The hooded man stood in front of Barry and talked in his muffled voice. "The end of your family at last, Sanderson. When the time comes, you shall know who I am and why I hated your father as I did. A lot of things will become more clear to you then."

Barry's hard eyes bored into the mask before him. He said: "One thing is already clear, you theatrical idiot. Fear is driving you. And your fear will catch up with you one day. Your fear will be your downfall. Build as high as you like. The whole thing will topple on the back of your neck."

He smiled contemptuously at Brisson. "Your little fat friend has more nerve than you. He's a swollen-headed fool in many ways. He has a touch of meglomania. You are altogether mad. Some day a man like Brisson will wipe you out of the picture. But I doubt if Brisson himself will do it. He isn't intelligent enough."

His face did not change as Brisson smashed his fist into the mouth that mocked him. Barry said to the hooded man: "You see, my masquerading idiot, you have a man that can't keep his head. I wonder if you can keep yours. I wonder if you are big enough to pull off the coup you are planning. Remember, there are a lot of policemen in America. The militia may surprise you."

Behind the mask laughter bubbled thickly. "Police! Militia! Do you think I haven't taken all that into account?"

The note of exaltation rose and swelled, giving a sharper edge to the voice, and Barry shivered. Somewhere he had heard that voice before. Then he forgot that mystery in the sense of what the hooded man was saying:

"Tonight will be the final stroke. Tomorrow police authority in America will be no more. Every city and town will be at the mercy of Brisson's men. We'll loot the United States as it has never been looted before. After that, Carthage will be President! Which means Carthage dictator! And behind Carthage, myself, directing the destinies of the continent. The Paladins will set up a new government in America. A government by—"

Barry knew that the hooded man had been on the verge

of uttering his own name. He had stopped himself with the name trembling on his lips.

"We must make our final plans," he said to Brisson. "These fools will keep for a while. Leave two men in the room with them as an added precaution. They are safe there. But we take no chances. You may underestimate them, Brisson. I never do."

THE DOOR SLAMMED hollowly behind them. Barry looked to one side at Grant. The one-eyed man smiled. His face was chalk white. But his good eye gleamed as brightly as ever. The big mouth twisted. "It was a swell game while it lasted," he said cheerfully. "I guess we had it coming. But we did slip some fast ones over while we were going."

Barry nodded. "And maybe we're not through yet." He turned his head and met Joe's stare. Something passed between the two. Joe nodded his head almost imperceptibly.

The two guards left in the room were in khaki shirts and breeches of the Paladin uniform. They held guns.

Barry leaned forward. His voice became very earnest. "What do you think you will get out of this? Do you think the big boss will cut you in on anything?"

One of the men was huge, with thick, sloping shoulders and a bullet head. "We cut in on the biggest take that was ever lifted," he growled. "Maybe you can offer us more?"

He turned his head and laughed shortly as he glanced at his companion. "Ain't that something," he chuckled. "Here are three dumb eggs in handcuffs and they ask me what I'm going to get out of all this. Monkey," he said to Barry, "you want to start worrying about what you're going to get out of this."

*"Fear is driving you," he said to
the hooded man, "and one day that
fear will catch up with you."*

Barry said, "There's an even million for you if you let us loose. An even million dollars."

The big man licked his thick lips and laughed again. "Where would you get a million dollars? And what good would it do us if we did collect? With the big boss in power, Carthage President, and Brisson running the big show, we'll have our hands on all the coin in the country. A million dollars is chicken feed, buddy."

Barry took a slow step forward. The slope shouldered man raised his gun and grinned ferociously. "Come right ahead, buddy. When you take another step I'll give it to you."

Both men were staring at Barry. The one-eyed man was tense, waiting. Joe stood like an image.

Barry whirled on his heel and jerked his head downward. "Go, ahead, Brisson," he snapped. "Go on, stare up here if you want to!"

Both guards turned their heads involuntarily and stared at the panel in the floor. They expected to see it open, with Brisson's face staring upward. But the panel was not open.

They whirled about as Joe launched himself like a projectile from his corner. His shoulder hit the slope-shouldered man and drove him into his companion. For a split second both men were off balance. And in that second Barry leaped straight toward the gun muzzle that was jerking up to meet him.

HE DID NOT take time to raise his manacled hands and dash them down. They came straight up to crash against the smaller man's chin. The man staggered back. He tried to raise the gun. But the manacled hands had completed their upswing, and now came crashing down across his forehead. He fell forward without a sound.

Barry's action had been swifter than the flicker of light. So swift that the one-eyed man made his first move as Barry swung from his own victim toward Joe. Both Barry and Grant halted and stared.

Joe had thrown his two hands over the slope-shouldered man's head. The chain that connected the handcuffs was across his throat. Joe's wrists twisted as he surged back, one knee in the middle of the big man's back.

The face of the slope-shouldered man turned purple. His eyes were popping from his head. His tongue was protruding and swollen against that inexorable chain.

Joe's shoulders gave a convulsive heave. There was a dull, sodden crack and the muscles and bones of the slope-shouldered man seemed to melt. He fell forward on his face as Joe flipped his chained hands back over the man's head and released him.

Grant's voice was awed. "I wouldn't have believed it if I hadn't seen it!"

"A matter of training," Barry said sharply. "We move just the fraction of a second faster than the other fellow."

Barry and Joe dropped to their knees and frisked the two men they had downed. There were no handcuff keys on them. But on the big fellow Joe found a watch.

Grant watched in something like amazed fascination as Joe smashed the watch on the floor of the cell. From the shattered case he picked a wheel and snapped it into halves with strong fingers. He tried one of the halves on Barry's handcuffs, exclaimed in exasperation, broke another fragment from the piece he had in his hand. He tried again, then rubbed the tiny fragment on the stone floor. It took him less than five minutes to fashion a makeshift key to unlock their manacles.

23

GETAWAY

BARRY LIFTED HIS head to listen. Below them a motor began to purr. He turned his head and stared at the high, barred window. Daylight was growing, making the light bulb over his head a pallid glow in the dim cell.

He stepped to the wall and snapped, "Up on my shoulders, Joe! See what that car means."

Standing on Barry's shoulders, Joe could just see over the sill of the barred window. His whisper was harsh and thin. "It's Brisson and the big boss. They're going away to push some of their plans before they come back to us. Give me that gun, Barry. Quick!— I can plug the fat rat. The boss is already in the car and it's got bulletproof windows."

He made a sharp exclamation of rage as he took the gun in his fingers. "Too late! He's in the car. There they go!"

He leaped to the floor. "Brisson and the big boss on the war-path. Bad! And it'll probably get worse."

Barry shook his head. "Think again, Joe. It's good. Now we can grab Carthage without Brisson and the big boss knowing it. They won't hurry the hour unless they know. Now they'll not know we're on the loose again. That's one in our favor."

Grant smiled. "We can make Carthage talk. I've got an

idea we can make him spill the works if we can get him alone for a few minutes."

The lock rattled. Someone was coming in. Which was what they wanted now. If they tried to pick the lock the guards outside would hear and be ready.

The door swung wide. Joe's fist lashed through the air as he struck the first man.

Barry brought the butt of his gun crashing down on the head of the second. Then he saw who was behind the two and went rigid. It was Elsa Darrow. She was clutching an automatic in her hand, an automatic that she had been jabbing into the back of the second man. Beside the door Barry saw the two sub-machine guns that the guards had dropped.

Elsa swayed on her feet and the gun slipped out of her hand. She caught herself, bit her lip and gasped, "How— how did you get loose?"

"We have our methods," Barry said dryly. "But you," he asked. "What are you doing here?"

"They were holding me in a room above. They took me to Baxter City with them. Then brought me back. The guard in my room got careless. I struck him over the head with a bronze vase and got his gun. I heard that they were holding you here. So I came to help."

"Your uncle," Barry snapped, "Moreland? Where is he?"

"I don't know. They kept us apart. I heard his voice a while ago. I think they were taking him away."

Barry nodded. He leaped forward to catch Elsa as she fainted. He held her for a second. Then he smiled thinly. "Let her stay out for a while," he said grimly. "She won't enjoy watching us work on Carthage. We'll bring him up here for the job."

CARTHAGE WAS AT his big desk, staring at the microphone in front of him. He felt a strange sense of exhilaration. In a few hours his voice would go booming out to arouse the nation.

It gave him a sense of transcendant power. He, Anthony Carthage, would be dictator of America. Of course there was the hooded man, who would be the real boss. But he would be the power on the throne. He wondered, almost idly, how long it might take him to have his boss killed.

Of course there was Brisson to figure with. Brisson was mad with a lust. Brisson would be hard to handle. Maybe the set-up was better as it stood. The three of them could handle the job that one man might not be able to swing.

Behind his desk the guard who never left him stood staring straight before him. These bodyguards who must be at his side day and night were symbols that Carthage, in his heart, hated. They were symbols of a life where death grinned and peered at all times. He consoled himself with the thought that when men like the three in the room above were dead the need for guards would not be so great.

He thought again of the cold muzzle of the gun that had driven him to the microphone to deliver the speech he had not wanted to deliver. That had upset plans somewhat. But in two hours he would go on the air again and repair that damage.

The smile that twisted Carthage's lips was terrible. He would enjoy watching those men die. They had cost him sleepless nights and fearful days.

He walked across the room and turned the knob that

controlled the sliding panel over his head. As the panel
moved, he walked back toward his desk. He wanted to
cheer himself with a sight of their helplessness. He tilted
his head back and stared up. His mouth sagged open, his
tongue and lips became paralyzed, trying to utter the cry
that would not come.

The man who came through the hole in the ceiling was
like an avenging spirit. His gray eyes were like polished
steel. His face was a rigid mask.

The cry came hoarsely from Carthage's dry throat as the
gun in the man's hand blasted and the guard against the
wall pitched to the floor. From the ceiling dropped another
man, a man with a face of pitiless bronze. Above a man lay
on the floor and smiled down; he had a black patch where
one eye should be.

The gray-eyed man known as Barry Chase was talking.
His words struck like white-hot irons on Carthage's trembling nerves. "It's the end of the trail, Carthage. Your little
dream of power is over."

Carthage's eyes jumped from one end of the room to the
other. At one end was the panel door through which Barry
had come when he was caught. The Indian smiled thinly.
He was squatted by the main door, his eyes on that panel.

He looked behind the desk to the secret door through
which the hooded man always came. The man above his
head chuckled. Carthage glanced up. The one-eyed man
had a big automatic in his hand.

CARTHAGE LIFTED HIS head and listened for some stir
of alarm among the guards. Surely they must have heard
something.

As though reading his thoughts, Barry said: "Too bad,

Carthage, that you made this room sound-proof. You can yell your head off and no one will hear you. And you will yell, Carthage. I promise you that. You'll yell or talk. I don't care which. I'm not a Brisson to torture for the love of it. I turn to the weapon only as a last resort. You have certain secrets we want, Carthage. You'll give us those secrets or some very horrible things will happen to you."

To Carthage it seemed that the world was tumbling around his ears. He knew that these men who faced him were implacable.

He shivered as he stood before the hard menace of the guns. He clenched his hands and tried to fight the panic that was rising in his throat to choke him. He was suddenly acquainted with a fear such as he had never known before. He knew it was showing starkly in his eyes, in the sag of his mouth, in the shuddering he could not control. He knew all this, and knew, at the same time, that he could not do anything about it. His guards outside suddenly seemed very far away and very puny and helpless.

Barry said, "Bring his chair from behind the desk, Joe. We don't want him to get near any alarm buttons."

When Joe came back with the chair Barry pushed Carthage into it. All thoughts of power and domination were gone now from Carthage. He was conscious of a world that had gone awry, of a great edifice that was falling about his ears, crushing him in its collapse. The death he had meted out to so many was very close and ugly and terrible.

In his brain a hammer of insistence began to beat. He would never leave this room alive. He knew that suddenly.

This office that had been his throne room would be his death chamber.

Even Grant drew back slowly at what he saw in Carthage's face. The vacancy of the eyes was mad. The slack lips began to slobber. Then suddenly Carthage began to laugh. Billows of mad laughter swept the room.

For a second Barry thought the man was shamming. Then, looking into his eyes, he knew the truth. Carthage had gone mad; stark, raving mad. He would never talk coherently again. The brain that had become warped plotting and building his dream of power had snapped. The sudden reversal had been too much for him.

"Watch him!" Barry said tersely to Joe and turned toward the desk. In the desk there might be some clue to those things that Barry must know.

He jerked out drawer after drawer without finding anything that helped him. He was fumbling with the edge of the desk when a thin board slid out.

Barry gazed at it and caught his breath. It was a map of the United States, with locations marked. These points, he knew now, were the concentration points where arms and ammunition were located. This was what he wanted.

He took the map from the board to which it was tacked, rolled it and slipped it in his pocket.

GRANT HAD GONE out. Barry and Joe went into the hall. Behind them Carthage was babbling in his broken, madman's voice. They climbed the stairs to meet Grant coming out of the room above carrying the limp figure of the girl on his shoulder.

Barry pushed the map into Grant's hand, saying sharply, "Take this and the girl and make for the nearest wire. Get the dope we have found to Washington. They'll have enough then to act on."

Grant stood for a second staring at Barry. "What are you going to do?"

Barry smiled gently. All the weight of worry he had carried seemed suddenly to have been removed. He said slowly: "The place is swarming with Paladins. We'll see that you get by them. After that we'll make our own break."

Grant reached out with his free hand and gripped Barry. "No matter what happens it's been a swell ride. After you two guys, any other partners would be tame. I just want you to know how I felt in case anything happens."

Joe slapped Grant on the shoulders as Grant passed out of the room. A squad of guards was racing up the stairs. A gun boomed and lead screamed past Barry's head. He lifted he muzzle of the machine gun and swept the stairway with a storm of lead.

He went down in front of Grant, sweeping the doorway with slugs, driving the panicky Paladins before him. Behind him he heard the chatter of Joe's machine gun and knew that the Indian was backing down the stairs, driving the men above back.

Barry threw himself down in the doorway and swept a hail of lead across the driveway. One of the guards at the gate swung around and fell. The other leaped for the safety of the stone gatepost.

"Now!" Barry snapped. "There's a car over there. Pray that there's an ignition key in it. Get going."

Grant crossed the yards in a driving rush while Barry's machine gun drove the Paladins outside to cover.

A slug whanged into the armor plate of the car and

screamed as it glanced off. Then Grant was inside the car, the girl swaying in the seat, himself behind the wheel.

For what seemed an eternity, Barry listened for the roar of the motor. Slugs from the guns of the Paladins were starring the bullet-proof windows of the car. He could see Grant bent over the wheel working desperately. Barry reached back and took the machine gun from Joe, who watched the interior of the house against a rear attack.

"Work with your automatic," he said hoarsely. "I'll need this. Mine is empty."

His heart sinking, he sprayed the line of bushes with lead and smiled grimly as a man screamed. And still the car motor did not start.

In the last desperate moment of waiting the motor caught with a roar. Gravel spurted as the wheels spun on the driveway. Then the big sedan shot through the gates and roared up the road in a cloud of dust.

Barry was breathing a sigh of relief when Joe ran past him out of the door. Joe reached a spot where a guard lay across his machine gun, jerked the gun clear and leaped back with it. "We'll need this," he said.

Barry said, "We'll go out through the cellar and make a break for the woods. Word of this will get to Brisson. We've got to find that fox before he gets away."

Joe halted Barry with a hand on his arm. "Listen!"

24

SUBSTITUTE PRESIDENT

IN CARTHAGE'S OFFICE someone was talking. Barry knew it would be into a telephone, tipping Brisson as to what had happened. He made a sign to Joe to hold the bottom of the stairs and raced up three steps at a time, He slid noiselessly into Carthage's office. Carthage was staring out of the window, babbling to himself of the kingdom that was to be his.

Another man was talking into the phone. "I tell you Carthage has gone nuts! He's raving, Yeah, the one-eyed guy got away with the girl. I don't know where the other two are."

"Here's one of them," Barry said softly.

The man slammed the phone into its cradle and whirled. He made a gesture as though to reach for a gun, then his hands came up slowly.

"You've got me," he said huskily.

"Yes," Barry said thinly, "your game is played out. Inside of an hour Washington will be warning the whole country. Where will I find Brisson?"

"I don't—"

Barry smiled. "You knew where to get him on the phone.

If you don't talk I'll call the Indian and put him to work on you."

"You're a pair of devils," the man said shakily. "No men could have done what you have done. I'll tell you."

"Very wise," Barry said. "You can save your life that way. Then you can go outside and tell your precious friends that the jig is up and the best thing to do is to scatter."

The man raised his head, "Brisson is in Baxter City. He's got a hide-out there in an old factory. The old Anderson Arms Company."

Bitter humor crept into his face. "I'd say that it would take a regiment to blast him out. But I suppose you'll walk in and drag him out."

Barry nodded. "We probably will. Now, I'll keep my promise. Go down the stairs and out the front door. Tell your men that they'll follow my suggestion if they're wise. I'll remember your face. If you get caught by the police I'll try to see that you get a break. Go on."

He followed him to the head of the stairs, calling to Joe, "Let this fellow go out the front door."

He came down slowly after the man had walked out into the crisp autumn sunshine. Joe said: "Hold this spot. I don't think anyone will bother us again. I'll dig up a bite to eat. Then let's get out of this. There's still a smell of something sour about this place."

In a few minutes they went through the passage that led from the basement to the woods beyond the grounds. The air was spicy with frost-touched leaves. The sunshine was clear and bright and warm. Barry drank deep breaths of the sweet air. It was great to be alive and out of that house of horror.

Beyond the house they could hear other motors roar into life.

"The rats are deserting the sinking ship," Joe said.

"Yes," Barry agreed. "But the biggest job is yet to do. We must find Brisson and make him tell us the identity of the big boss. He is the only one who knows. Carthage knew, but the secret is locked in his mad brain."

THEY SAT FOR a few moments in the wood, eating bread and cold chicken and drinking milk that Joe had found in the kitchen. Barry gazed at Carthage's watch tower, that great stone monument to the maddest plot the country had ever known.

The enormity of it staggered him. All over the nation the machinery was in motion. Nothing but swift action on the part of the police and militia could head it off. And to get swift action they must all be warned. Also, they must be informed of the location of Carthage's arms caches. Otherwise Carthage would be the front for a terrible dictatorship of murder.

The plot might still succeed if Grant failed to reach a wire with his news. It might still succeed in a measure if Brisson remained at liberty. Brisson and his boss might at least pull off part of their coup—the looting of banks left unprotected by the disorganized police, which Carthage claimed Brisson and his gangsters would do before Carthage and his Paladins took over thereby reaping untold riches.

Barry knew now that he must find the Unknown, and unmask him and bring his career to an end, so that he, Barry, might be Gerald Sanderson, a free man for the first time in as long as he could remember.

He bent his head listening. He could hear the shouts

of men who fled on foot and knew that the watch tower was deserted. In a very short time, if Grant were successful, government men would take charge and gather all the secrets that the stone tower contained.

But even as he looked, the great tower suddenly burst outward and dissolved in a cloud of smoke. The roar of the explosion made the earth tremble. The tortured air roared like a gale through the trees around them. The sky above seemed to shudder. Then smoke drifted lazily down the wind and silence poured back into the bowl of destruction to wipe out the titanic noise that had ripped the quiet countryside briefly asunder. In the other of it all was a heap of smoking ruins. And under it somewhere was the body of Anthony Carthage, the man who had dreamed of dictatorship of America.

Joe shivered. "I had a hunch that something like that would happen. I felt it in my bones all the time I was in the place. We just got out in time."

"Brisson!" Barry said thinly. "They must have had the place mined for just such an emergency. I'll stake my life that Brisson had a wire to Baxter City."

Joe flung away a cleaned chicken leg. He rose and stretched, then smiled at Barry. "Lead on!"

ALL THE BRIGHT flippancy had gone from Brisson's voice as he sat at the desk in the old factory and talked to the hooded man across from him.

"Carthage is gone. And we don't know whether Chase and his pal were blown up with him. I think they were. But Casden hasn't got back yet. Why doesn't he get here?"

The hooded man said hollowly: "Get a grip on yourself, Brisson. We've received a blow. That shouldn't upset you altogether. The thing to do now is to make sure that we go through to the goal that has not changed substantially."

Brisson's mouth twitched. He looked at his hands rather than at the man across the table. "If we only knew about those three," he said thickly. "If we knew that they were dead, things would shape up differently."

"You make me a little sick, Brisson," the hooded man went on. "You've let these fellows get under your skin. I thought you were made of different stuff. I didn't expect much of Carthage. He was just a windy demagog, a tub-thumper, without courage. I had imagined you had both. I had believed that I could count on you till the last ditch."

"You can!" Brisson's voice was almost a snarl. "I've got what it takes. I'll see this thing through. But you can't blame me for wishing I knew. Once I know that they are either dead or alive I can make my plans. I'll stick. And we'll ride through to a grand finish!"

"That's better," the hollow voice said with a touch of something like relief in it.

Both men stiffened as the buzzer on the desk cut through the silence. The hooded man leaned forward and snapped a switch.

"Yes?"

The flattened voice of the annunciator said, "Casden reporting."

"Good! Send him in." The hooded man straightened as he snapped the switch off. "Now, Brisson, you'll know. I am as relieved as you are. We'll know. And we can make our plans accordingly."

Casden's face was grayish and pasty. His eyes were shifty

and full of fear as he came into the room. He stared from Brisson to the hooded man.

Brisson's voice crackled in the silence of the room. "Well, why don't you speak? Why stand there like a dummy? Did Chase and his two men get out of the tower before it went up?"

Casden nodded. He swallowed, slowly, painfully, as if he found it difficult to speak. Then his voice came strained and flat. "Yes, they got away. They went out before the tower went up."

Brisson swore in a flat monotone. "That's what I get for giving you a break, Casden. I held the switch long enough for you to get out. And while you were getting out those ghosts went too."

"Your solicitude for Casden deserves commendation," the hooded man said bitingly. "Since when, Brisson, have you developed such thoughtful consideration for the lives of your helpers?"

"I wasn't thinking of Casden, alone," Brisson snarled. "I gave him the break because I thought those nosey fools would go through the place looking for documentary evidence. I was certain they'd give the joint a thorough overhauling."

He paused and stared at Casden. The man's mouth opened wide, a gaping orifice that writhed and twisted as he tried to find words to beg for mercy, to plead with Brisson for the break he knew he would not get. For he saw death in the eyes of the little fat man. And it clutched his heart with icy fingers, paralyzed his vocal chords, gripped him so that he could neither speak nor move for a long few seconds.

Words and motion came back to him in the same instant. He took a step forward, arms outflung imploringly. "Don't, Brisson. Don't!"

BRISSON PULLED THE trigger of the automatic. Casden jerked, raised high on his toes as though reaching for something, then spun around and fell. Brisson shot him three more times as he went down.

He stood, staring down at the dead man, his lips drawn back from his teeth, his fat cheeks twisted, his eyes horrible in their rage.

The voice of the hooded man jerked him back to the present. "What does that get you, Brisson? Casden was a good man. He had as much nerve as you had. Perhaps more. But he talked. Make sure that you do not talk when the time comes."

"I'll not talk," Brisson said thickly. "Chase and the Indian will come here. I'll see that they never leave. I'll make sure of it this time."

Brisson slipped the gun back under his armpit.

"Now," the hooded man said in a changed voice, "let us see what we have to do. Carthage is a martyr." Irony edged the muffled voice. "We can spread the word that the enemies of the Paladins, the lawless element who menace law and order, have struck down the great leader of the people. We'll yank Roberts from Chicago and put him in Carthage's shoes. The Paladins will be all the easier to lead since their great Carthage has died a martyr to their cause."

Brisson nodded. "That's good logic. Roberts can be President just as easily as Carthage could. And he'll be an easier man to handle. I never trusted Carthage. Once he had gotten into the saddle he might have got ideas of bossing the show himself."

"Obviously," the hooded man said. "I knew that. And I had made my arrangements accordingly. I choose my lieutenants with open eyes, Brisson."

Brisson shivered a little at the implied threat in the muffled voice. The hooded man seemed to sense Brisson's fear. Cold humor flowed from the man in the robe.

His muffled voice continued. "Roberts will be the standard bearer for the Paladins. Have your men strike as soon as it gets dark. Washington cannot act in time to head us off now. Our plans have been too well laid. Wreck the militia barracks and police stations and there will be nothing Washington can do. We can laugh at them while we marshal the Paladins to take over the enforcement of law and order. Everything will go through in spite of Washington."

"I'll take care of my end," Brisson said. "I'll see that the raids are carried out on schedule. The key men in the Paladins will see that the arming of their men is carried through. That has been so well planned that it can't be stopped." The sound of his voice seemed to give him fresh confidence. Something of the bright mirth seemed to flow back into his pink cheeks. His red lips curved in a smile and his blue eyes gleamed sharply.

"That's better," the hooded man said. "I thought for a moment that you had lost your nerve. You can't do that now, Brisson. Only nerve will carry us through. If we keep that nothing can stop us. Chase and the Indian have hurried us. But fortunately we were ahead of schedule on the movement of arms and ammunition. Fortunately your men had carried out orders so well that law enforcement was already tottering. One last push tonight and it will break down beyond all hope of repair."

Again the annunciator buzzer cut in on their conversation. The hooded man threw the switch. "Yes?"

"Chicago reporting," the annunciator crackled. This time there was panic behind the voice. "Militia have just raided the headquarters of the Paladins and arrested Roberts. They have seized all papers. Secret Service operatives are going through them now. The ammunition and arms for the Paladins was seized also."

The box was silent. The hooded man reached out a steady hand to throw the switch when the voice went jerkily on. "Flash from Brisson's headquarters in Chicago. Local police re-enforced by militia made a swift and terrific raid on our men. In a fierce battle dozens killed and headquarters taken. All men not killed, rounded up and taken to jail."

"The crack-up!" Brisson said hoarsely.

25

BRISSON MEETS JUSTICE

"SHUT UP, FOOL!" the hooded man said harshly. "Don't let the first adverse stroke stampede you. Chicago isn't the only city in the country. They can have Chicago."

"But Roberts has been arrested," Brisson said hoarsely. "Won't he squeal his head off?"

"After tonight it doesn't matter," the hooded man said. "Besides there are ways of shutting a man's mouth even in prison. I shall see that a lawyer is sent to Roberts. After that Roberts will commit suicide. Dead men can't talk, Brisson. You said that yourself."

Brisson nodded. His face was dull and flat again. He shivered at the sneer in the hooded man's voice.

"You're a weak-kneed coward, Brisson. All your nerve is surface show. When the real test comes you start to crack up. Keep a grip on yourself. We'll come through this all right. Even without the Paladin coup we can loot this country clean. With the money we'll take, building the Paladins back to power will be easy."

The voice in the annunciator came on again. "Paladin Headquarters at Detroit raided. Militia in charge. Police raid of Brisson headquarters now in process. Terrific fighting going on. Will report as soon as definite results are known."

"Those three damned ghosts," Brisson said harshly. "They are responsible for this. They sent the word to Washington and got this action. But how in hell could Washington move so fast?"

"Washington can still get action once they are warned," the hooded man said quietly. "The success of our plans lay in the fact that they were shrouded in mystery. As long as Washington didn't know what we were planning they were powerless. Now they know and the fight is in the open. Everything hinges on our men now. They have an even chance. They have better than an even chance. For they are well armed and must go through if they want to go on living. We have desperate men fighting for us, Brisson. I like desperate men."

He raised his head and seemed to be studying Brisson. "I like desperate men who don't lose their nerve."

Brisson moved uneasily. A cold-hearted killer himself, he feared this man as he feared no one else. His fear of Barry Chase and the Indian was a different fear. It was mixed with the fierce hunger to torture and slay.

The hooded man went on: "As for Chase and the Indian, we shall have to fix them. There is more than mere hatred between them and me. I knew Sanderson, Brisson. I hated him, Brisson. I killed him and the mother of his pup. Someday I shall kill the pup."

With his gaze on the desk, Brisson remembered Barry's voice. It was beating on his brain with hammers, telling the hooded man it was not hate, but fear he felt. The hooded man had feared the elder Sanderson. He had killed him because he had feared him. Because he had feared Dirk Sanderson he had searched until he had found him in his hiding place in the hills. And, in finding him he had found the younger Sanderson grown to manhood, a man trained for a job; dedicated to that job.

Then, Brisson knew, the hooded man had begun to fear the boy as he had feared the father. It was all part of the same pattern of fear and hate.

Brisson lifted his head. His world was a world where fear and hate were the ruling passions. Men had their hates and ambitions and let those emotions drive them. But the ruling passion was fear. Every man had his fear, and that fear governed his life and the end thereof.

The annunciator cut in on his thoughts. "Marines and sailors landed from the fleet to reinforce all police in coastal cities. Boston: Paladin headquarters raided. Marines and sailors with local police made a clean sweep of Brisson headquarters. Surprise attack caught men unprepared. Many surrendered. Many killed. Only a few escaped. These being hunted by police who are raiding every known hang-out."

THE HOODED MAN leaned forward and snapped the switch. He stood up with his hands beneath his cloak.

"You're right, Brisson," he said huskily, "it is the end. Now I shall have to start over again and build another organization. Next time, however, I shall use more care in choosing my men. I shall pick lieutenants with nerve; men who won't crack up at the first sign of trouble."

Brisson stood up. His legs trembled. He put both hands on the desk to support himself. His eyes were blank and empty. They looked at the hooded man as Casden's eyes had looked at him, Brisson, just a few minutes earlier.

"You can't do this, Chief!" Brisson gasped. "We're in this together. We can pull out of it together."

The hooded man shook his head slowly.

"You are the only man who knows who I am, Brisson. You are the only one who has ever seen my face. Look at it again, Brisson. Look at it again."

His left hand lifted the mask from his face. Brisson stared, his eyes blank, his mouth sagging, a little trickle of saliva flowing from his lower lip.

The sight of the face seemed to give him back some of his nerve. He jerked his hands from the desk and his right leaped to the holster under his arm. His hand was touching the gun butt when the gun under the black robe barked.

Brisson's hands dropped back to the desk. For a second his arms stiffened, propping him up as life flowed out of him. His face tightened, screwed into a grin of agony. Then it smoothed out. His eyes had a look of blank surprise.

The hooded man let the mask drop in front of his face. He walked around the desk and stood for a second staring down at Brisson.

He opened the door and heard no sound. Under the mask his lips twisted in a sneer of contempt. His men, like rats, were deserting the sinking ship. Well, let them. The show was over. The only thing to do now was to get away; go back to life again and forget the death that had been so close to him. He stripped the cloak and mask from him and tossed them aside.

THE OLD FACTORY at Baxter City was deserted when Barry and Joe entered with Militia and police hours later.

They found the switch that had set off the explosives that had blown Carthage's watch tower into oblivion. Doubtless Carthage himself had never known that the big boss had held that trick up his sleeve, that at any time he could have blasted Carthage from the face of the earth if that wily demagog had decided to grasp the authority for himself.

Joe was the first to enter the office where Brisson and the hooded man had held their last conference. He glanced into the room and turned his impassive face to Barry and said, "You said you'd catch Brisson if you had to chase him to hell. Well, you might as well start your trek to hell at once, Barry. You'll not catch him short of there."

He watched Barry's immobile face as he stared silently at Brisson, and Joe's dark eyes glowed with a deep and fierce fire.

Captain Custer of the Baxter City police came into the room and stared from the dead man on the floor to Barry and Joe. Something he saw made him shiver.

"I begin to understand what it is you two fellows have. I hope you never take the warpath with my scalp as the goal."

A voice behind him said, "Checkmate!" and brought Barry whirling around.

Grant Page was standing in the doorway. His one good eye gleamed sharply, and his ugly face was split in a wide grin. He stepped forward and gripped Barry's hand and slapped Joe on the back. "Good hunting! I got the word you sent in and beat it back here."

He stared at Brisson's body and said huskily. "I don't get my wish. Well, I guess it's just as well. I might have been ashamed of myself afterward."

"By the way," Grant said, "the girl is back in New York.

I got her a plane and she flew to New York. I reported her return to Washington. Her uncle was picked up along the road. I just got that word from Washington. They say he's in bad shape."

He paused and smiled. "The girl is half-crazy worrying about you. I'll call and tell her you're all right. She wants to see you as soon as you can make it."

Barry turned with a start as Joe handed him the black robe that the hooded man had cast aside. He took it and turned it over in his hands. He spread it out on the table and studied it. On the inside of the front were stains, still wet.

He stared out of the window for a second with unseeing eyes. Then he said slowly, "I'll go see Elsa now. Dig up a plane, Grant, and we'll start."

Grant frowned. "We should head for Washington first. Why New York and the girl?"

"Brisson and Carthage are dead," Barry said flatly. "Everything is under control. There's just one more thing to do. Let's go."

26

THE WAY OUT

FROM THE LANDING field in Newark they motored into New York. The city seethed with excitement. Newsboys screamed the latest information in the streets. On every corner the blare of radios could be heard through open doors and windows as the broadcasts of the latest evidence was given to the waiting people.

The tenseness of frightened expectancy was gone. Pedestrians walked more freely in the streets. It was a city that had been freed from a bondage of fear; of a dread that had chained men and women for long months.

The butler who came to the door of the Moreland home told them that Miss Darrow had gone out. But that she would be back shortly. He evidently had been told of Barry Chase and was expected to keep him should he call while Elsa was out.

In the lower hall Barry said, "We'll go up and see Mr. Moreland while we're here."

The butler said, "I'll see if the master is awake and will see you."

He went up the stairs on feet that made no sound, to come back as noiselessly and say, "Mr. Moreland is awake, sir. He is most anxious to see you and thank you for all you have done."

Joe and Grant would have stayed behind but Barry said, "You'd better come along with me."

He halted in the door of the huge bedroom. Moreland was propped up with pillows. His fine eyes were turned toward the door waiting for Barry to enter.

Barry walked across the room, his hand outstretched, his lips curved in a smile.

Moreland smiled gravely. "Well, my boy! It's splendid to see you again. How are you, Mr. Sanderson? Or do you still insist on Chase?"

Barry gripped Moreland's hand. He heard Grant's gasp as he jerked Moreland forward in the bed, tore back the bedclothes with a sweep of his hand and knocked the gun out of the hidden left hand.

"The name from now on is Sanderson," Barry said harshly.

"I don't get it," Grant said in a husky voice.

All the life drained out of Moreland's face.

Barry's voice cut like a whip through the heavy silence of the room. "You were my father's best friend, Moreland. You posed as his best friend and hated him as one man should never hate another. You had started your criminal career then. When my father got on your trail you got jittery. Fear was added to your hate, so you killed him. You killed him and my mother!"

Moreland shivered at the icy bleakness in Barry's tone. He looked at the faces of the two others and knew that he could expect no mercy. The one-eyed man's face was like stone, still and cold and hard. A mask of impassivity had dropped over Joe's face. Only his eyes were alive; black eyes in which the fires of hell were dancing.

Moreland knew in the clarity of that instant that he could not escape. And suddenly he knew also that he wouldn't want to escape it now if he could. He was through. The game was played out.

In that instant he thought of Elsa. "I want you to know, Sanderson," he said slowly, "that Elsa had no part in this."

BARRY NODDED. "I know. You used her for a pawn. You used the only thing you loved. You let me see her that day back in the hills and figured that I would walk into your trap if she were the bait.

"I should have known then. The way you were imprisoned by Skelton was a beautiful move. But I should have known. I should have noticed that the handcuffs you wore when you went in were not locked. You slipped them off to kill the two men who were with you, and Skelton when he began to crack.

"You had planned it well. You had a man below in the car ready to drive away at a signal. All you had to do was throw up the window after the shooting and toss the gun into the car. Then, while the car drove away you gave your head a bang and snapped the handcuffs on your wrists again. That was clever, Moreland. And now you are through."

"Yes," Moreland said huskily, "I'm through." He sat up straight in bed, his big hands clutching the bedclothes. "But I led you all a dance before I finished."

His voice took on a note of gloating triumph. "If I'd had a few men as smart as myself I'd have beaten you all. But I didn't have them. All I had was a demagogic fool and a shrewd sadist. Yes, even with such material I shook the foundations of a continent."

He paused and stared at Barry with eyes that now took no pains to hide the flaming malevolence. "Yes," he said in a voice that was as dry as paper, "I hated your father. I hated him. And I killed him and there isn't a thing you can do about it. Oh, yes, you can kill me. But that will be weak revenge and you know it."

He stared from Joe to Barry and went on. "I hated him all his life. I hated him because he won everything. In school he was the brilliant leader. I loved your mother. But she married your father. When you were born I knew that you were the son I should have had. And you belonged to the man I hated.

"I worked into crime because I found a world where my brains could be utilized to better advantage than anywhere else. I built the house of crime that baffled even your father. When he began to get too close I killed him. I wanted to kill every one connected with him. I hated Dirk as I hated his brother. I wanted to kill you.

"Because of that I never rested till I had caught up with you. I killed your uncle. I killed your friends. I came near killing you."

BARRY SAID: "AND for all your scheming and murdering and plotting what have you now? You're an old man, and you've got to die in disgrace and fear. Because you're scared of me, Moreland. Don't lie. You're afraid of me as you were of my father. You're shivering right now down in your black soul. You're crawling like a snake now. You're a rat and you're due for a rat's end, Moreland."

"But you won't kill me, Sanderson," Moreland said, and

his voice was sharp with triumph. "You wouldn't dare go
to Elsa with my blood on your hands. I know you and your
kind. You poor, puny Galahad."

"I don't want to kill you, Moreland. If it were not for
Elsa I would call the police now and see you pilloried in
the scorn that every honest man would feel for you. That
would get you, Moreland. It would curl you up inside to
hear the mobs howling for your blood."

He saw Moreland shudder and knew that he had scored
a point. He went on relentlessly: "But because of Elsa I'll
not do that. I'm going to give you a break, Moreland. It's
a break you don't deserve. But Elsa has that much coming
to her."

He held Moreland's gun on the palm of his hand. "I'll
give you this gun as we go out, Moreland. You can fix
things for Elsa. It's the end for you. But you owe the girl
something. You have dragged her around in your dirty
game. You've used her for a pawn. You've hidden behind
her skirts. Now you can square things for her. No one but
the big boss in Washington will ever know your story. I'll
see to that. You can die honored and respected. Or, you
can pass up your chance and go the other way, through the
gutter to the grave of a rat."

The three of them backed slowly toward the door. Moreland watched them go with his empty gaze. Something
on the faces of the three men chilled him as nothing had
ever chilled him before. The thing that struck hardest was
the biting scorn. They had played against him and he had
lost. But in their faces was none of the admiration that a
winner feels for a good loser. He had been something else,

a loser who loses because of the game he plays. And this was the end.

Barry tossed the gun from the door. It landed soundlessly on the bed beside Moreland, who looked at it a long moment vacantly. His hand was just reaching for it as Barry closed the door.

The butler was waiting for them in the lower hall as they came noiselessly down the stairs. He stared from one face to the other. He felt baffled and a little frightened by what he saw in the three faces.

His voice quavered, "You saw the master, sir?"

Barry bowed. "Mr. Moreland is greatly upset by all that has happened. He has undergone a frightful experience in the hands of the men who held him and Miss Darrow. I would watch him carefully if I were you." His impassive face conveyed only a sense of concern and sympathy.

The booming shot in the room above sent the butler scrambling up the stairs. The three men waited till he returned. His voice cracked and wavered. "He did it, sir. Mr. Moreland shot himself. What shall I do, sir?"

"Call a doctor," Barry said. "And notify the police. It will only be a matter of form. But I would do that."

"Right. Quite right, sir." He hesitated. "About Miss Darrow, sir. It will be a most terrible shock to her, sir."

"I'll wait for Miss Darrow," Barry said evenly. "I wish to see her."

Half an hour later Barry heard the taxi stop in front. He could hear Elsa's swift footsteps up the walk to the door. "I'll handle this," he said to Grant. "Stick around for a few minutes and wait for me."

His heart quickened as he saw her coming toward him,

her hair gleaming like gold in the light from the door, her eyes shining, her hands out-thrust in quick welcome.

THE FOLLOWING DAY the three of them stood in the White House and shook hands with a grave-eyed man who smiled and whose voice trembled a little as he thanked them for their work.

"I hope," he said, "that you two volunteer members of our force will not quit as abruptly as you appeared. Men like yourselves are hard to find."

Barry smiled. "We hope, sir, that the Department will call upon us whenever the need arises."

From the White House they went to General Jeffery's office. The man who met them was not the strained and harassed individual who had talked to Barry on that day that was so little distant in the past, yet felt to all of them as if it were years ago.

"Thanks to you boys," General Jeffrey said, "we've got everything under control. We've rounded up the ringleaders and put the fear of the Lord into the hearts of the rank and file of the Paladins. We've made the biggest harvest of criminals that was ever made in history."

He paused and stared at the three of them for a moment. "Brisson and Carthage are dead. We've got all their lieutenants behind bars. We've got everyone but the man we want the most, the man who engineered the whole thing. No one in the Department has a clue to his identity. That's what I wanted to talk over with you today. Are you going to stick till we get him?"

Barry's face did not change expression. "We came in to quit now, General. We got your man yesterday. Rather, he got himself when we caught up with him."

"He got himself?" General Jeffery repeated blankly. "But—Moreland," he gasped. His mouth closed with a snap. "But that's impossible, man. Moreland was working with us. He was in on everything."

"Exactly!" Barry said tersely. "That's why he was so successful in his plot. It was Moreland, all right. He admitted it when we caught up with him. That's why he committed suicide."

General Jeffery got up from his chair and walked to the window. When he came back his face was very grave. "That closes the case as far as you boys are concerned then. Does anyone else know this?"

"Only we four—and—" he hesitated—"Elsa Darrow, Moreland's niece."

Grant looked up with a start. Joe did not move. "But you said you were not going to tell her," Grant gasped.

"I didn't tell her," Barry said slowly. "She guessed. She had begun to wonder when she was used so well by Brisson and Carthage. When she saw me and heard that her uncle had committed suicide she knew for sure."

Barry met General Jeffery's eyes again. "We five are the only ones who know. Don't you think it would be better for all concerned if it went no further?"

"Certainly," General Jeffery said briskly. "It would do no good to publish the news. Business men all over the country are today looking upon Moreland as a sort of martyred member of their class. It would shake the confidence of the country if the truth came out. By all means keep it a secret."

His care and worry seemed to drop from him. His gaze came to rest on the one-eyed man. "I suppose," he said smilingly, "that you'll want to take a long vacation, Grant."

Grant nodded. "I've had my fill of man-hunting for a while. I'd like to go up into the hills somewhere and shoot a few grouse, eat and sleep and rest and forget the whole nightmare."

"I know just the spot, Grant," Joe said, smiling. "Come along with Barry and me."

Barry said, "It will mean a hold-up for a few days. I want to start the move to establish my identity. It won't take long. I've got all the papers."

"Leave that to me," General Jeffery said. "I can put all that through for you. Leave me your papers and go on your trip. You've all deserved it."

Joe looked at Barry a second before he said softly, "How about Elsa Darrow? Where does she fit into the picture?"

Barry's lips curved in a smile. "Don't worry about her, Joe. We've talked things over. After what has happened she wants to get away and sort of let things blow over. She's leaving in a few days on a world tour. The hunting trip appeals to me right now."

He let his smile travel around the faces of his friends, and he said softly, "Our hills, Joe. They'll look very peaceful and lovely after what has happened. It seems like years since we left them."

Grant stood up and grinned. "Wait till I get my glass eye put back in my head. You'll like me then. I'm pretty as a picture when I get my glass eye in place."

The three of them walked to the door together. Watching them, General Jeffery shook his head. "If there's ever another nightmare such as we've just been through," he said softly, "I hope there are men like you around to call on."